The King of China

TILMAN RAMMSTEDT

TRANSLATED BY KATY DERBYSHIRE

LONDON NEW YORK CALCUTTA

This publication has been supported by a grant
from the Goethe-Institut India

Seagull Books, 2019

Originally published as *Der Kaiser von China* by Tilman Rammstedt
© DuMont Buchverlag, Cologne, 2008

First published in English translation by Seagull Books, 2013
English translation © Katy Derbyshire, 2013

ISBN   978 0 8574 2 731 1

British Library Cataloguing-in-Publication Data
A catalogue record for this book is available from the British Library

Typeset by Seagull Books, Calcutta, India
Printed and bound by WordsWorth India, New Delhi, India

The King of China

THE
SEAGULL
LIBRARY OF
GERMAN
LITERATURE

For Marianna

There is plenty of room between the folds of Buddha's skin.

Chinese saying

My grandfather was dead by the time I got his second-last postcard, but I couldn't have known that. I'd put it aside unread, just as I'd put all his previous postcards aside unread. Almost every day they lurked in my letterbox amid the bills and circulars and then formed an increasingly precarious pile under my desk, which I covered with an old newspaper. Not that it helped much—I knew perfectly well what was hiding underneath.

For the past ten days, almost everything had been taking place under my desk. I crawled round on all fours, my knees padded with washing-up sponges, venturing only into parts of the room not visible from outside. I slept under my desk, I made myself sandwiches there, I drew a night sky on the underside of the tabletop and waited for the two weeks to pass, for me to be credibly back from China, so that I could find some kind of explanation for what needed explaining—one explanation for my grandfather, one for Franziska and one for my brothers and sisters, provided they hadn't discovered me by that point. I had to come up with something as quickly as possible, so there was no time for postcards. They'd just have to wait, and my grandfather, I believed, would have to wait too, and then came the phone call and there was no need for waiting any more.

I hadn't answered the phone, of course—I hadn't answered the phone for ten days by that point—but I heard a woman on the answering machine asking me to call back. 'It's urgent,' she said, but I had an idea that it wasn't true, that I was dealing with the most un-urgent thing in the world. I called back nevertheless, and my grandfather turned into a dead grandfather, his postcard turned into his second-last postcard and I turned into something very confused and very monosyllabic. 'Yes,' I said a few times, and 'No,' and 'Fine,' but nothing was fine, because although I had one less problem to deal with there were now plenty of new ones, and I hung up, plucked the second-last postcard from the pile and believed I was sad.

On the front of the postcard was a statue of a fat man seated on an elephant in the middle of a golden flower and the back was once again crowded with my grandfather's tiny, gnarled scrawl. I'd always found it difficult to decipher but now, I discovered, it had degenerated into absolute illegibility. Even through a magnifying glass, I couldn't make out any recurring words, nor even identify the vowels. By the time I gave up trying, I'd unearthed a 'fine', a 'mountain' and a 'morning' or 'moaning' or 'moving'—I wasn't quite sure which.

Only the last sentence was written clearly, larger than the rest and in capital letters like the address, etched so deeply into the card that their mirror image protruded from the elephant on the other side. 'You should have come with me,' they said, and my grandfather had added a wedge-shaped exclamation mark after them to convince me once and for all that his words weren't a mere polite phrase, an expression of affectionate regret, but a severe disappointment, an accusation, a threat. And because this was now his second-last postcard the threat rang out all the more, as if he wouldn't have died if I'd accompanied him, as if his heart wouldn't have stopped all of a sudden, or if it had, then at least in China, but best of all not at all. If I'd gone with him all he'd have had to do was hold on to me briefly—'Nothing, I'm just a bit dizzy,' he'd have said—and I'd have taken him to a park bench and bought him a bottle of water because I wouldn't have come up with anything else, because nothing else would have been necessary. 'I'm fine now,' my grandfather would have said a few minutes later and taken out his comb—his greatest concern would have been his hair.

'You should have come with me'—how those words annoyed me! I heard him saying them, emphasizing the 'should have', his eyebrows arching downwards, looking at me afterwards as if he expected an answer, the right answer of course—Yes, you're right, Grandfather, I should have gone with you, it was a mistake, you're right as usual. My grandfather liked being right. My grandfather had always known everything beforehand, or so he claimed— you should have taken an umbrella, you should have looked at the map, you should have learnt more lan- guages, you should have washed that shirt separately, you should have ordered the steak. My grandfather was always offended when no one had listened to him, but no one could listen to him because he only ever told you what you should have done differently after you had done it. But no one ever asked him, he said, and now look, you're all wet, and now look, we've got lost, and now look, I'm dead.

Yes, I should have gone with him, and no, I hadn't gone with him, and I knew it looked as if I'd abandoned him, I knew it looked as if I'd betrayed him and I also knew I could have explained it all to him somehow, but now there was no need for that any more. And I didn't have the slightest idea whether it was appropriate to be relieved.

It was plain to see that the second-last postcard didn't come from China either. It had a German stamp on it and the picture of the fat golden man had been torn out of a travel brochure and stuck slapdash over a free postcard, one corner already come unstuck, revealing a polar bear underneath. Almost all the cards my grandfather had sent me over the past few weeks had been adapted that way, sometimes not even that. Some of them had pictures of mediaeval churches on them and the printed text 'Greetings from the Westerwald Mountains' had been partially crossed out and replaced with a handwritten 'Shanghai'.

Of course, I was hardly surprised that my grandfather hadn't made it to China after all. Eight thousand kilometres—the car was too old for such a long trip and my grandfather too was too old for such a long trip. Most of all, he'd have needed a passport, and it seemed my grandfather didn't have a passport with him, no identity card, no driving licence, not even his loyalty card from the supermarket. They hadn't found anything on him, the woman had told me on the phone, only a half-written postcard with my name on it. And why couldn't he have finished writing it? Why couldn't he have just popped it into a postbox? Then no one would have called me, then I could have imagined him having a great time in the car—probably chatting to an attractive hitch-hiker he'd picked up at some picnic area or other—then I wouldn't have to get to the

Westerwald as quickly as possible to identify my grandfather. And then I wouldn't know how far away he still was from China in the end.

China—China of all places, as if there was no North Sea coast, no Harz mountains, no Rügen island, no France, no Lake Garda—it had to be China; China and nothing else. 'I don't want to discuss the matter,' my grandfather had said, and I'd said that suited me fine because I didn't want to discuss the matter either; China was out of the question. And I folded my arms and my grandfather did too. Actually he only had one arm, the right one, but he could wrap it round his left shirtsleeve so cleverly that it looked as if he had two intact, folded arms. And then we gave each other a long stare, my grandfather as determined as possible and I as derisive as possible, to show him what an absolutely ridiculous idea China was, and then my grandfather said, 'I'm going to die.'

That's not a sentence to be taken too seriously, not in retrospect either, not even now that my grandfather had proved himself right once again. So I said, 'You're not going to die,' although, of course, that was a lie whatever the case. But I didn't want to allow his line of argument, I didn't want to be made into the person who turns down last wishes, I wanted to stay objective because in objective terms I was in the right, of course, and China was absolutely impossible, but being in the right is no use when it comes to dying people. My grandfather knew that and so he'd started dying early just to be on the safe side. My grandfather, you see, had been dying for as long as I can remember, probably even longer, and he only stopped doing it just before he died. My earliest memories of him are he giving me a serious look and saying, 'Soon, I won't be here any more,' and then pointing at all sorts of things I was to inherit after his departure—the oil painting of the galloping horses, the dagger-shaped letter opener, the rotary ashtray—all the things we admired at the time. I found out years later that he'd promised my brothers and sisters the same items, with the same conspiring winks, with the same 'This is our little secret.'

I never confronted him about it because firstly, the painting and the letter opener had long since lost their appeal and secondly, we'd grown used to reacting to my grandfather's announcements of his impending death with nothing more than a nod. No one in the family bothered to contradict him any more, no one said, 'I bet you'll live to a hundred,' because it seemed more and more likely that he really would live to a hundred. Every visit to the doctor, always preceded by long leave-taking rituals, confirmed my grandfather's almost sinister constitution. Up to a few months ago he had all his own teeth, up to a few months ago he only needed glasses for reading and, even then, he usually did without them for reasons of vanity. Despite what started as countless cigarettes and went on to be countless nicotine chewing gums, his lungs and heart were still in tip-top shape for many years and it probably wouldn't have surprised anyone if his left arm had grown back.

But then his body finally noticed that this state of affairs was inappropriate for his age and over a remarkably short time it caught up on what it had previously neglected. Muscles went limp, arteries congested, joints swelled up, ears grew. From then on my grandfather brought home a new medication from every visit to the doctor. Where once he'd had the occasional half a tablet next to his glass at mealtimes, now the line began to stretch along the entire width of his plate. 'Oh yes, my dessert,' he'd say before he picked them off the tablecloth one by one with trembling fingers and swallowed them, grimacing with disgust. My grandfather made perfectly sure that the rest of us were watching, that we saw exactly what he was putting himself through. Sometimes he dropped the odd tablet, presumably deliberately. 'No, no,' he'd say when one of us went looking for it under the table, but he made no attempt to bend over and accepted the rescued tablet without a word of gratitude.

And, in fact, it was my grandfather's failing health that prompted us to give him the trip as a gift. 'Who knows how much longer he'll be fit to travel,' my eldest brother had said, and the rest of us hadn't come up with any better idea. One week over the Whitsun holiday, and we'd all take a few days off; we'd survive if we did it together. But then, first my elder sister jumped ship, saying something about a project week, then my second-eldest brother, saying something about a tight deadline, and seeing that it wasn't going to be a trip with all of us grandchildren anyway now my younger sister suggested we draw straws. 'Then not all of us will ruin our time off,' she said. And my straw was the shortest, there was no doubt about it. The other two didn't even try to hide their relief. My younger sister clenched her fist in a moment's triumph and my eldest brother slapped me on the back rather too hard. 'Keep your pecker up,' he said, presumably meaning to encourage me, but it sounded like a command. Did they think it was such a good idea for me, of all people, to go on holiday with our grandfather, I asked them, but the others waved away my objections. 'Perhaps it's really best this way,' they decided unanimously, 'then the two of you can spend some time together after all these years.' That was precisely what I was afraid of.

It was impossible to tell whether my grandfather was pleased with our present, which had now become more like my present even though the others would pay their share—absolutely, they assured me. He had studied the gift certificate and then put it aside just as expressionlessly as all the other gifts—the framed family photo, the cognac, the Marilyn Monroe book. 'Keith is going on a trip with you,' my second-eldest brother explained, his voice once again rather too loud and rather too jolly, as he'd been talking to my grandfather all the time recently. 'We'd all have liked to come along but you know how it is.' And of course my grandfather didn't know, how could he have known, he was too busy running his tongue along his teeth, something he'd been doing non-stop since he'd got his dentures, and he looked at my second-eldest brother uncomprehendingly.

'A trip to where?' he asked after a while.

'Wherever you've always wanted to go,' said my younger sister.

If only she hadn't. For, the next morning, still in his pyjamas, my grandfather said 'China,' and he was still saying it that lunchtime, and he said it again that evening, and when I showed him some brochures—Prague, Poland,

Corfu—he didn't even look. 'China,' he said. 'A gift's a gift,' he said. And he said he didn't want to discuss the matter and then he folded one arm and then death was brought into it.

'And even if you were going to die,' I'd said, 'that'd be one more reason not to go to China. China's a long way away, China's hard work and none of the doctors in China would understand you.' And my grandfather had smiled— that sad smile of his that no one could imitate—and he said in that case he'd prefer not to go at all and he wished me a good trip to Corfu and immersed himself in his Marilyn Monroe book. And I stood there longer than I wanted to and watched him put his index finger to his tongue every time he turned the pages, with an implausible frequency. 'Whatever you say,' I said, before promptly leaving the room, and the house, and getting as far away as possible.

It was now early in the afternoon, or at least that's what the radio alarm clock said, the one I'd installed under my desk and on which I occasionally listened to music, my ear pressed to the speaker turned low. I myself had lost all sense of time. I slept during the day as well, as much as I could, and then I was disappointed to find it had only been half an hour. I had promised the woman on the telephone I'd leave immediately. That was more than five hours ago, so one or two more wouldn't make much difference.

I began to pack a few things. I wouldn't need much because I wasn't intending to stay long. A brief glance would suffice—I'd nod and then my grandfather would be pushed back in his drawer into the shapeless wall refriger- ator. I'd seen it all before in films. It would be a large, bare room, blankly lit by neon tubes, the pathologist wearing a white coat, of course, and averting her eyes discreetly. 'I'm so sorry,' she'd say, not even attempting to sound genuine.

And perhaps it'd even be better to wait for another night to let everything settle a little, perhaps today would be too soon, perhaps I wouldn't even recognize my grandfather today. Or perhaps he'd start going on about China again, even now.

He'd never been to China of course; he'd hardly ever been anywhere. As it turned out, he'd never actually left the European continent, never left Germany, had only come quite close to the Dutch border on one occasion and once, to put it generously, neared the Danish border. He had never paid a bill in a foreign currency, never had to ask anyone if they understood German and, apart from a few words of English comprehensible only to himself, he spoke no foreign languages.

'And why China of all places?' I'd asked him on the phone the day after his birthday. He'd been calling me almost non-stop since eight o'clock, telling me that I should pack plenty of good deodorant because it was hard to find in China, that I'd need a decent pair of shoes, and asking if I'd had a malaria vaccine. 'For God's sake, you've never even been to Austria,' I exclaimed, and my grandfather said nothing, said nothing for a long time, for so long that I asked, 'Are you still there?'

'Yes,' he said. 'I don't want to go to Austria,' he said. 'I've got no time left for Austria,' he said. And now it was I who went quiet because, in fact, if I thought about it, I didn't want to go to Austria either, at least not with my grandfather. If I thought about it, I didn't want to go anywhere with him, not up a mountain, not to a beach, not to a desert, not to a museum, not to a spa. I didn't want to spend longer than necessary flicking through bilingual menus with him, to silently enjoy views with him, to claim to be exhausted from all the walking at a ridiculously early hour over an evening glass of wine just so as to prevent any opportunity to spend time together. And perhaps, if I thought about it, China was the only sensible suggestion because even bilingual menus would be of little help there because you'd probably really be exhausted over an evening glass of rice wine, because it wouldn't be so bad there not to get along with each other because you couldn't get along with anything else either. And there was probably much too much of everything there, except for time for spending together, and in the best-case scenario you wouldn't even know what to use that time for. And, all of a sudden, I remembered how I'd thought my grandfather was Chinese for a few days when I was a child.

He must have been arguing with one of my grandmothers as usual, I can't remember which one; in any case they were very noisy and at some point he shouted, 'Oh yeah? And I'm the King of China.'

At the time I was less impressed by his royal office than by his origins, and I told everyone I knew but not everyone believed me. Why didn't I look Chinese, I was asked, and I replied, 'I will,' although I had no idea what Chinese people actually looked like. They all looked the same, I was told, and I imagined a country crawling with versions of my grandfather, where my grandfather was driving every car, where my grandfather stepped out of every house every morning and said goodbye to my grandfather, ready to take his children, five very small grandfathers, to school. The truth came to light a few days later. 'You're not Chinese,' I said to my grandfather.

'Whatever you say,' he replied.

Back then I'd liked the idea of a country full of grandfathers but now, on the telephone, it seemed like a horrifying prospect. One grandfather was enough for me, one grandfather was actually more than enough, and that was the issue here, not China or Corfu or Austria.

'Are you still there?' he asked me now.

And this time it was I who said, 'Yes, I'm still here,' and then hung up.

I'm not sure how many of my brothers and sisters I'm actually related to but I can safely assume that I share at least one parent with most of them. I can still vaguely remember my younger sister being born. I was four at the time and all of us went to visit my mother in hospital. 'There you all are,' she called out in a voice still a little weak, but it later became clear that she had to think about my second-eldest brother's name for a long time, and she kept looking at my elder sister very tentatively as well, as if she wasn't quite sure if she'd seen her before somewhere.

So I can only infer that that woman in the hospital was my biological mother, but apart from biology we didn't have much to do with each other at the time. I lived with my grandfather from a very early age, whereby I can only infer that he's my biological grandfather, of course. There's a certain similarity between him and my mother: their chins, their short fingers, and that will just have to suffice—he always evaded any more detailed questioning. Once, I found a photograph of him as a young man with a girl on his shoulders and I asked if the girl was my mother. He took the photo, gave it a glance with his eyes screwed up and then handed it back to me and said, 'Probably.'

My grandfather thought many things were probable— that we had milk in the fridge, that the summer holidays were coming soon, that the water went down the plughole the other way round in Australia. He holed himself up in his probabilities, sometimes even giving the respective percentages. You could never be quite sure of anything, anything at all, he taught us, and if one of us piped up with a contradiction, he'd add, 'Except that you'll die. That is indeed very probable.'

But he seemed to see a tiny chance of even that not happening and in the past months, since his body had been catching up on its age-appropriate decline, he had clutched at that tiny chance with a perseverance I'd never known he had. His ambition not to die had gradually become a full-blown obsession. Every few days we had to accompany him to the cemetery, where he paced along the graves with triumphant exclamations of 'Younger', 'Much younger' and 'Almost the same age', and if anyone had had the temerity to die at a mature age he noted down the precise dates, which he then copied into the list above his desk. Seventy-nine years two hundred and eighty-two days, eighty-one years six days, eighty-eight years one hundred and twenty-nine days. He'd overtaken some of the people on the list in the past few months, crossed out a few more names, and then he gathered us all up. 'Congratulations, Grandfather,' we chanted.

But he waved away our birthday wishes. 'Thank you, but I've not achieved anything yet.'

His wish to outlive everyone else soon began to take alarming forms. Death was not only his adversary; it also became his helpmeet. He would read out the death notices with relish over breakfast—'That was a good weekend'—he'd gaze hopefully after every ambulance that drove past, he developed a suspicious penchant for disaster movies, and it was only at the last moment that we prevented him from burying my younger sister's tortoise in the garden one afternoon. 'It was clinically dead, honestly,' he claimed, ignoring the tortoise's legs struggling visibly in the barely ankle-deep pit.

There were moments in the past few months when we were seriously concerned for our safety. If one of us as much as coughed, my grandfather instantly pricked up his ears—'That doesn't sound good'—and it wasn't worry that resonated in his voice. I'm not sure whether I was imagining it but the suspicious incidents came more and more often. He kept topping up my eldest brother's wine glass even when he'd stressed he had to drive; my elder sister reported scratch marks on her hairdryer cable; and as I was carrying a crate of mineral water down the steep staircase to the cellar a few months ago, my grandfather suddenly turned off the light. 'Sorry,' he said when I shouted a complaint up the stairs but he didn't turn the light back on.

It was around this time that my grandfather began accusing me and my brothers and sisters of being after his blood. There was constantly something wrong with his medication, he claimed, we were constantly putting butter in his food although he was supposed to watch his cholesterol, someone was constantly opening the window to make him catch his death. 'But it won't work on me, my dears,' he'd say. 'Not me, oh no.'

My grandfather did know, of course, that he very probably wasn't immortal and never would be, despite all his efforts and precautions. I suspect he was stubbornly hoping to get too old to die one day, to be at some point simply forgotten by death, the way you hope the telephone company will forget you once you've ignored all their bills and final demands and the telephone line simply goes on working because no one knows someone is still using it.

And it is indeed hard to imagine that he's supposed to be really dead now, that he's brought his life to a complete end, because he never brought anything else to an end. In the old days when we still had grandmothers, some of them an appropriate age, some only a few years older than us, they would keep telling him—one after the other and in almost identical phrasing—to finally finish something off, for God's sake: his tax return, the pergola that had been unintentionally two-tone for years, the jigsaw on the living-room table that we'd even stopped noticing or at least the name for the cat. 'Friedrich or Vincent' is still written on its wooden cross in the garden.

My grandfather would always nod in agreement, sort through a few receipts or add a jigsaw piece or two and then quickly look for something new to do—the furred-up coffee machine, the tangled phone cable, cards for birthdays some time in the future—anything he could claim was much more urgent.

And because my grandfather never finished any of these new activities either and had to find new ones as excuses for these, his entire house, his entire life consisted of beginnings. Everywhere, you'd come across books lying open, half-eaten sandwiches, single shoes, you'd hear stories that broke off mid-sentence, mid-word, the names of almost all our past grandmothers still written on our letterbox, and sometimes, after he'd announced he was going to bed, you'd bump into my grandfather standing in the hallway half an hour later. 'I'm on my way,' he'd then say quickly.

Where on earth was I, asked the woman from the hospital on my answering machine. Her voice sounded as if she was making an effort to be friendly, and I heard something in the background that sounded like a saw, but I hoped I was just imagining that. She'd be there until six o'clock herself, she said, and the night shift knew I was coming. And I was to bring my grandfather's passport along, of course, or his identity pass, birth certificate, some kind of official proof of identity. Before she hung up she added, 'See you in a bit then, I hope.' She almost sang the last word, as if we had a dinner date that she'd been looking forward to for ages.

The travel-information line informed me that the trip to the small town in the Westerwald would take an hour and twenty minutes with one change of train. My grandfather had been on his way to China for a good two weeks and now I didn't even have to book my ticket in advance. The trains ran every two hours, as I'd found out as well. 'Thanks,' I'd said, then clambered back under the desk and fished out of the pile the postcards my grandfather had sent me since his departure. I found eleven of them, not knowing if that was all nor remembering the order of their arrival. I looked for some kind of sign but everything remained illegible. All I could decipher was a few words, parts of sentences that annoyed me because of the lack of context. 'Polystyrene' annoyed me, 'antipasti platter' annoyed me, 'but a good body feeling again' annoyed me even more—none of it told me anything, none of it interested me.

I didn't know exactly what kind of sign I was looking for. But my grandfather must have known he wouldn't make it to China, that he'd be lucky to make it to Austria without any ID, and they hadn't found any ID on him; he must have thought it wasn't necessary. No matter how stubborn he could be, he must have known he wouldn't get far under those circumstances, and if it hadn't been the Westerwald, then some other forest, some other small town, some place else that you couldn't mistake for China with the best will in the world, and China had then been out of the question at some point, even if he hadn't wanted to hear it. 'Of course we're going,' he'd kept saying, sometimes several times in a row, sometimes so quietly that he couldn't have been talking to me at all.

Over the past few years his eyes had flickered in increasing panic whenever anyone contradicted him and his face took on something cold and stiff with increasing speed, so that none of us dared to look at him directly. He never really resorted to violence; only broke the occasional piece of crockery. Usually, he twisted his right arm round his left shirtsleeve several times, presumably to prevent anything worse, and we left the room as fast as we could.

'Grandfather's moods', as we called them, were always followed by long phases of silence, of staring, of motionlessness. He'd sink down in his armchair and respond to our cautious questions with a 'Mmh' at the most, to be interpreted as rejection or agreement by its tone alone. He'd stay away from family meals, and what he presented as regret was presumably intended mainly to garner our sympathy. 'But you've got to eat something,' we'd say willingly enough, acting concerned although there were plenty of indications that he made himself sandwiches or helped himself to our leftovers as soon as we turned our backs.

My grandfather was not a great cook himself, no matter what he said. He usually found something to complain about with the food our grandmothers or we made, adding generous amounts of salt before he even tasted it and then telling us for the entire length of the meal how he'd soon make us a stew or a joint of boiled beef that would 'make your ears wobble', as he put it. It never came to that, naturally enough. Once he gave us a long, detailed shopping list but by the time we got back from the supermarket he had gone missing and remained so until he sat down at the table for dinner that evening without a word.

If we had visitors and they praised the food, he was always the quickest to thank them for the compliment. When we confronted him later, he'd say he had meant it on behalf of all of us. Apart from that, though, my grandfather was like a whole different person in other people's company. He did still talk a lot but more quietly than usual, and often about the subject we were actually discussing. He asked questions and waited for the answers, he laughed genuinely, even at other people's jokes, he didn't enquire apparently innocently whether someone 'didn't want that any more', only to launch his fork across the table and help himself from their plates. There was no choice but to find him charming, at least when the guests were women, especially if they were young women, and most of all, if they were young women I'd invited.

What a delightful man my grandfather was, I heard often enough. How entertaining he was, I was told. So young for his age, so attentive and what a gentleman, they said. And some of them even used the word sexy. Whenever these young women came to visit for a second time the house smelt of my grandfather's eau de cologne from the early afternoon, he often changed his shirt several times and sometimes he'd even get her a little something—the book the young woman had feigned interest in the last time, a small porcelain elephant if she'd mentioned she liked animals and, after several visits, perhaps even a brooch that he claimed matched the young woman's eyes.

The more often the young women came to visit, the fewer opportunities my grandfather missed to make a fool of me in front of them. It began with harmless childhood stories, went on with unflattering photos from my early teens and culminated in outlandish lies—that I still wet the bed 'now and then', for example, or that I'd worn my sisters' dresses as a child, remarkably often. It was possible that what was planned as a romantic date at the cinema or a cafe was suddenly interrupted by my grandfather sitting down next to us, bumping into us ostensibly by chance—'I hope I'm not bothering you,'—which could only be explained by him having secretly followed me. My distraction manoeuvres got more and more complex, I whispered our arrangements more and more incomprehensibly on the telephone and spent our romantic dates looking round more and more frantically, so that in the end they were our last dates.

No wonder I stopped bringing women home at some point and made a secret of any closer acquaintance with girls. The result, however, was that my grandfather thought I was suffering from social isolation and constantly wanted to go out and do something with me. 'Let's go to the theatre tonight, just the two of us, just like we used to.' He'd present the idea with such enthusiasm that he wouldn't even notice my attempts to turn it down. 'But you love the theatre,' my grandfather would say, although that wasn't true in the slightest. It was my grandfather who loved the theatre or at least claimed so. In a lofty voice he'd recite the only lines from *Faust* that he knew by heart, 'The ancient one I like sometimes to see.' 'Goethe,' he'd exclaim, 'Goethe drank five litres of wine a day. A genius,' and when I sat alongside him in the stalls, in the Caucasian chalk circle, in the cherry orchard, in Tauris, he'd fall asleep at the latest after the double helping of sparkling wine in the break—'Aren't you drinking yours?'—and didn't wake up until the final applause, often with threads of saliva in the corners of his mouth. Then he'd stumble to his feet, still slightly dazed, for a one-man standing ovation and shout 'Bravissimo' so loudly that he'd have me heading for the cloakroom in embarrassment.

After the play he'd ask me to show him a bar, an 'in-bar', he specified, but as I had no idea what he meant by that we always ended up in Pete's Heavy Metal Joint, where he drank half a beer out of the bottle, clearly intimidated, and stared at the label on the bottle for a long time between sips. 'I'm tired,' I'd say out of pity after a while and he'd nod with relief.

On the way home he'd perk up a great deal though. How lovely an evening with just the two of us was—'Yes, Grandfather,'—at last we'd found time to talk to each other—'Well, Grandfather,'—I should bring one of my girlfriends home one of these days—'There isn't any girl right now, Grandfather,'—I could always ask his advice on that kind of thing—'Thanks, Grandfather,'—he thought we had rather similar taste when it came to women—'Could be, Grandfather.' We didn't know back then just how similar that taste could be. We didn't meet Franziska until a few years later. Before she was my lover, Franziska had been my last grandmother.

'So, where are the two of you going?' Franziska had asked me after I'd persuaded her to come home with me after all, following my grandfather's birthday dinner.

'Not to China, that's for sure,' I said.

'Plenty of other places left then,' she said, checking the time on her mobile phone and looking for her car keys in her handbag. 'I've got to go,' she said then, far too soon.

At the door I said, 'Drive carefully,' and meant something else and she just gave a tired smile and I closed the front door quietly but not until I couldn't hear the last sound of her engine any more.

The previous night, Franziska had suddenly leapt up. 'What am I doing here?' she had said and dressed hastily, and I had sat up in bed sleepily and told her I'd like to know that too and that she ought to lie down again quickly, and Franziska gave me an angry look. 'I could be your mother,' she exclaimed as she looked for the boots she'd tossed aside in abandon a few hours back.

'But you're not,' I said. And because I couldn't be sure of many things in my family I asked, 'Or are you?' and Franziska laughed out loud.

'God forbid,' she said, 'although it'd hardly make things any worse.' She couldn't take all this mess right now, she added. 'I really can't,' she said, and then she found her boots, pulled them up to her knees with both hands and looked at me. 'Aren't you going to stop me?' she asked, and I wondered for a moment whether I was going to, whether I could actually take all this mess right now and whether everything would be less of a mess without Franziska. 'Yes,

I am,' I said in the end, once Franziska had reached the doorway.

'Hurry up then,' she said and ran out of the house, and I tried to catch up with her but by the time I got to the road she was already in her car. Naked and shivering, I stood on the cool road surface as Franziska wound the window down. 'That was close,' she said and I wondered how I was supposed to stop her, how on earth I could possibly hurry up enough to meet Franziska's expectations. No one was as fast as she was, she was forever waiting for you, forever turning round to look back at you, forever ending your sentences for you because she not only talked faster but also listened faster than other people, she heard things that hadn't even been said yet, sometimes not even thought.

'How should I know?' she answered now too, before I'd said anything out loud, and wound the window up again. 'Make me a proposal,' she said then with a half-hearted laugh and drove off at her usual speed, the tyres screeching at the corner. I knew that sound well, just like her delayed gear change at the next road, and I stayed standing there even after it faded away, my arms crossed against my chest as if that would protect me from something. And of course I wasn't relieved, of course nothing was neat and tidy now that she'd obviously gone. The mess with Franziska was nothing in particular compared to all the mess I was used to from my family, you see, and then, the next day, I drew the short straw and my grandfather said 'China', and there was nothing neat and tidy in my life at all.

If you believed my grandfather's stories, which was rarely wise, Franziska had always been fast. For six years in a row, he claimed, she was a youth sprinting champion and she set some record or other in her old age group that was unbroken to this day. I didn't know if that was really true but I could well imagine it.

Things supposedly couldn't go fast enough for her from the very beginning. She was born premature by two full months but still learnt to speak and walk before the age of one, according to my grandfather. She was sent to school early only to skip two years, I think the sixth and the eleventh. My grandfather had forgotten how many semesters she'd taken to sail through her law degree. 'It was a ridiculously small number, anyway,' he said with a proud smile.

She usually evaded the issue when I asked her about her past. 'It's always such a long time ago,' she'd say, then screw her eyes up a few times and change the subject.

The postmark on my grandfather's second-last postcard was hardly any more legible than his handwriting. A sorting office that wouldn't tell me anything anyway and a date, the 18th or 19th, but that made no difference now. He was no doubt still alive at that point and he was no doubt no longer alive now, and there was almost as little doubt that he hadn't known he'd die, so there was no reason for him to tell me anything more important in this postcard than in his countless other ones. All those postcards all that time, even when we'd lived together in the house. He'd put them in our letterbox without stamps, only to bring them to me at the breakfast table with a triumphant 'Post for you, Keith!' Even after I moved out to the garden house the postcards didn't stop, sometimes arriving several times a week, now sent properly by post although it would have been much easier, of course, to simply put them in my letterbox, but we'd come to a tacit agreement to regard the few yards between us a serious distance. Most of the cards showed aerial views of our town. He bought them in folding ten-packs with visible perforations along the edges. Now and then he opted for an art postcard, melting clocks or black-and-white photos of naked backs or clothed washing lines. I didn't always bother to read them.

It wasn't just the cards, though, that earned me the dubious reputation among my brothers and sisters of being his 'golden boy'. They taunted me as 'Grandfather's pet', as his 'son and heir' and 'the apple of his eye'. For myself, the preferential treatment over all the years was usually unpleasant. Before it began there had been a kind of doctrinal sense of justice between us, adhering to which was tiring in the best case and a health risk in the worst. We all got exactly the same presents for Christmas and for birthdays, although at that time all we had anyway—so as to avoid temporary bias—was a single celebration referred to as 'the family birthday', which had been fixed as the twenty-fourth of June so as to be as far removed from Christmas as possible. We successfully rebelled against uniform clothing but my grandfather nevertheless made sure our wardrobes consisted of the same number of items which were, as far as possible, equally expensive, with the price difference paid out immediately to those at a disadvantage.

Things got unpleasant when my younger sister got her longed-for ballet lessons and we all had to take part in the classes. Even more unpleasant was my second-eldest brother's stubborn ear infection, when his antibiotics were shared out equally between all of us. Fortunately, none of us broke any bones during that time.

But the older we got, the more we resisted my grandfather's efforts not to put any of us at a disadvantage. My older brothers and sisters had already entered adolescence, which created biological injustices for which my grandfather couldn't find any compensation. It's not quite clear whether it was out of resignation or a genuine change in his thinking that he finally gathered us for one of our then-still-regular family meetings and explained to us that he unfortunately didn't have enough energy to devote himself to all of us equally, so he had decided to concentrate on taking care of me to avoid being left with a collection of mediocre individuals in the end. 'That doesn't mean I don't still love you all the same though,' he told us, and he made us swear we believed him.

It wasn't until years later, without my ever asking him, that he revealed why he had chosen me. My older brothers and sisters, he told me, had simply been too old 'to get anything major sorted out' and he claimed he'd always been a little sceptical about my younger sister. 'She's not really true to type,' he said in an almost scared whisper, as if there had ever been a type in our family to be untrue to.

Ever since that family meeting, he had taken me on a little outing every weekend, to the zoo, to the science museum, to endless piano recitals, and then related all the details to the rest of the family over dinner while I stared mutely at my plate, studiously avoiding my brothers' and sisters' eyes. He helped me patiently with my homework, and displayed every essay that got a good mark on the fridge door, even if he'd written most of it himself—more as an admonition to the others than as a reward for me.

Later came the long walks. 'You're a very special boy,' 'You're going to make something of yourself,' 'You won't disappoint me, Keith, I know you won't.' When I wanted to be an astronaut at the age of eight he gave me a telescope. When I wanted to be a secret agent at the age of ten he signed me up for various martial-arts courses and we installed bugging devices in my brothers' and sisters' bedrooms. Then when I wanted to be a filmstar at the age of thirteen he dragged me from one audition to the next. You can see me running along a road in an ancient TV series, my only ever on-screen appearance. 'You're the best runner, absolutely,' said my grandfather but by then it wasn't as important to me.

From the age of fourteen I didn't want to be anything any more and my grandfather chose my passions for me. Architecture, pyrotechnics, 'something with computers'—unread books on the subjects still fill entire shelves. 'You've got lots of different interests, that's the thing,' my grandfather decided and I didn't contradict him.

Of all this special treatment, the postcards remained the most unpleasant though, particularly over the past few weeks—when my grandfather would have had more than enough reasons not to send me any more, although I wasn't quite sure if he knew the reasons.

Sometimes I thanked him for the postcards but I never sent one to him. I kept trying, kept writing 'Dear

Grandfather,' sometimes adding 'Thank you very much for your card,' but then everything got stuck, nothing occurred to me to write next, nothing seemed worth telling him. The half-written postcards piled up in my drawers, many of them fully addressed, some already with stamps on them, their value or currency no longer valid. Why I never threw the cards away I don't know. Perhaps I thought it was a waste—after all they were almost unused. Or perhaps I just didn't want to admit my failure to myself, that I hadn't managed to write even a few banal lines to him in all the years, that I persuaded myself there wasn't space on a postcard for what I thought I wanted to say to him, even though I didn't know exactly what that was and how much space would be adequate.

And now, now that all the space in the world wouldn't be adequate because not only the stamp but also the addressee was no longer valid, I took one of the half-written postcards out of the drawer.

Dear Grandfather,

it said already, in much too large letters, presumably in the hope of filling a considerable portion of the supposedly inadequate space with the salutation alone, which was of little use because four-fifths of the card was still blank. And all at once I didn't want to put up with that blankness any more, all at once it seemed more than a failure, for perhaps the space had always been adequate, perhaps it had even been too much, perhaps there had never been anything more to say than 'Dear Grandfather,' perhaps even the 'Dear' was exaggerated, and perhaps I should have sent all the cards off just as they were—that would at least have suited the circumstances. But now the circumstances were different, conclusive and clear, and I picked up a pen and wrote under the first line,

You are dead.

My handwriting had barely changed in the years between the two lines. I'd then used a black pen and now used a blue one but there were no other differences.

Then I wrote,

Best wishes,
Keith

and stared at the six new words for a long time. There wouldn't be any more.

In the first few days under my desk the phone had hardly ever rung but now it hardly ever stopped. I kept hearing my voice on the answering machine, I kept holding my breath because I suddenly wasn't sure if the callers could hear all the sounds I made and because I was afraid my game of hide-and-seek might come crashing down round me thanks to a stupid technical hitch.

This time it was Franziska. Her calls had started ten days ago, as I'd expected. 'It's me. Where are you?' 'This is Franziska, call me back!' 'Don't tell me you're really in China, are you?' 'Hello? Oh, shit.' Sometimes she didn't say anything and all I heard was her footsteps, on floorboards, on linoleum, on cobbles, in such a rush that they could only be Franziska's.

'This is getting silly,' she said this time and then added in a slightly lower voice, 'I have to talk to you urgently, Keith.'

Franziska had never used my real name before. That was the first thing she promised me, the first thing she ever said to me.

'This is Franziska. You'll be seeing a lot of each other from now on,' my grandfather had said when he first brought her home for dinner, and we tried to remember her name even though we could never be sure what 'a lot' meant with my grandfather's lady friends. Franziska walked all round the table and shook each of our hands.

'I'm Keith,' I said when she got to me at the end.

'Really?' she asked. I nodded and Franziska stroked my arm pityingly. 'I'll never call you that.'

From then on she called me Special K, sometimes Mick if she wanted to annoy me, now and again What's-your-name—which she thought was funnier than I did. And when she said 'I have to talk to you urgently, Keith,' it was the broken promise that shocked me more than whatever was supposedly so urgent. The woman from the hospital had said something about 'urgently' as well, and my brothers and sisters were constantly saying 'urgently'—'I need it back urgently,' 'The car urgently needs fixing,' 'You have to get in touch urgently as soon as you arrive in China.' But in all the confusion I simply couldn't work out which of these things was really urgent, which of them was very urgent, which of them were undeferrable and which might be less urgent if I waited long enough, because by then it would be too late anyway.

And the longer I inhabited my hiding place under the desk, the greater the temptation became to pick up the phone after all, to say, 'Hello Franziska,' to say, 'Yes, I'm back again now,' or even, 'No, I'm not back again because I never went away in the first place.' In all this confusion it would do me good to have a quick word with someone other than myself. It would do me good to tell the truth again at last too, but I couldn't let myself give in to that temptation. Otherwise it's all too easy to get worked up about things and then you blow your cover or everything comes tumbling down. For a moment I'd be relieved, I expect, before I realized that I'd still have to explain myself despite everything. I owed a good few people explanations either way, so they might as well be the kind that didn't mean I was showered with accusations, the kind that wouldn't prompt uncomprehending shakes of the head, screaming and perhaps tears, probably even sober silence. So if I wasn't going to get away without explanations, they might as well be the kind that everyone would be happy with in the end.

15 May, Beijing

My dears,

Grandfather and I landed in Beijing yesterday after a journey of fifteen hours and twenty-five minutes. The flight went fine, despite grandfather alerting the cabin crew to alleged noises on several occasions. He didn't fall asleep until the captain had personally assured him that he was perfectly capable of flying in the dark.

From Capital Airport, we then took a taxi for the twenty-seven-kilometre journey to the centre, which cost approximately eighty-five yuan. On the way, Grandfather asked the name of almost every building we passed but the taxi driver didn't understand German, not even very loud German, and then Grandfather soon gave up and kept saying 'Well' or 'That'll be something or other,' and chewing his nicotine gum.

We're staying at the Bamboo Garden, a cosy and tranquil hotel. The staff aren't quite as helpful as we'd like but that has partly to do with the culture, Grandfather explained. The rooms are tastefully decorated, Ming furniture, a small but clean bathroom, abundant foliage outside the window, but Grandfather says the typical flair of the old city is somewhat restricted by the modern residential block directly opposite. The room costs 680 yuan, a mid-range price as we found when we made a comparison.

Grandfather and I went for an evening walk round Dongcheng (that's the name of the area where we're staying), past the East Church with its large square up to the hill of Jingshan Park, from where we enjoyed the magnificent panorama of the capital and an unparalleled overview of the russet roofing of the Forbidden City. The last of the Ming emperors is said to have hanged himself in this park as rebels swarmed at the city walls. Grandfather was very moved by this story. A couple of rebels and bam!—a whole dynasty comes to an end, he said with a shake of his head.

In the evening we ate out at Baguo Buyi, a Sichuan restaurant as good value as it is popular, decorated in marvellous Chinese-inn style. The ambience was bursting with both character and theatre. Grandfather chose *zhacai rousi*, deep-fried pork or beef filet with brown mustard, and I decided on *ganshao yan li*, boiled carp with ham in sweet and spicy sauce, which Grandfather preferred to his own dish so we swapped after a few bites.

The only problem was the chopsticks. They only put on all the hocus-pocus for tourists, Grandfather said, no one had been eating with them for centuries. Even when I showed him that all the other diners, almost entirely Chinese, were uncomplainingly and skilfully consuming their dishes with these 'antediluvian' implements, he waved away my objections. Tourists, he said, they're all tourists.

In the end I ordered a knife and fork for him, and every time I dropped a morsel into my bowl he gave a mocking laugh and raised his glass, 'Here's to civilization.'

Grandfather is asleep now. I've been looking for an Internet cafe but haven't found one. Apparently they've been closing down one after another here in Beijing, so I'm writing this by hand and I'll send it as soon as I can.

All my love,

K.

It was easy for my brothers and sisters, of course. They acted all the more generous now that everything would be slightly more expensive than planned, but they were still prepared to distribute the travel costs equally. The older ones would even cover my younger sister's share because she couldn't afford it, after all. 'China,' they said with twinkling eyes, I was a lucky bugger, they'd all been dreaming of going there for years, and they said things like 'exciting' (my eldest brother), 'stimulating' (my elder sister), 'something a bit different' (my younger sister). And I said I'd be happy to let someone else take my place if they were all so envious, but they just shook their heads sadly. They didn't have time right now, they regretted and then they smiled. 'You go, don't worry,' said my elder sister.

And my second-eldest brother said, 'Yes, you really deserve it.' He didn't say why it was I who deserved it.

And my grandfather remained equally insistent, although I had hoped he'd stop mentioning China after a few days, stop mentioning the whole trip in fact. Most of the gift certificates that circulated in our family never got cashed in anyway. But not a day passed when he didn't talk to me about China, when he didn't put some newspaper clipping or other about China in my letterbox, when he didn't manage to divert every conversation to 'China' after three sentences at the latest. Did we know that gold was called 'yellow salt' in China, he might ask out of the blue at the dining table, or when my second-eldest brother set out for his evening walk, my grandfather might claim that, interestingly enough, jogging was absolutely unheard of in China, and he might confirm arrangements you were trying to make with him with 'So you mean half past five, Beijing time.'

The simple obstinacy of the first few days gave way to a frightening earnestness. He actually lugged home piles of brochures, looked into offers for cheap flights, and one morning I even found a gift-wrapped travel guide outside my front door, with the line 'China really has something to offer to everyone' underlined and annotated with two exclamation marks in the margin.

He now even started finding understanding replies to my flimsy excuses. He thought it admirable that I was taking my studies so seriously but I'd soon catch up on a couple of weeks' absence; in fact, the only way I'd miss something important was if I didn't go to China with him. He made it more and more difficult for me to disguise my refusal as the only sensible attitude, with me slipping more and more into the role of the obstinate one. 'The whole China thing is a ridiculous idea, isn't it?' I asked Franziska one evening, despite having actually promised not to mention the subject again. And when she only shrugged noncommittally instead of instantly agreeing, I told her not to start too and wondered out loud why everyone was suddenly so obsessed with China, why everyone was suddenly talking about nothing else, and why they didn't all go to China together, they could immigrate there for all I cared, if it was really such a fascinating country, but they should leave me in peace with their China. Franziska said,

'Don't you worry,' and that she'd leave me in peace all together, and she went to the door.

'I won't stop you,' I called after her.

And Franziska called out, 'Fine,' and said I'd never manage that anyway.

And I called out, 'How could I anyway?' and told her she was so terribly flighty that no one could keep hold of her.

And Franziska said that I was the right one to talk, 'the world's most prolific procrastinator,' and I could at least have inherited that from my grandfather. 'At least he knew what he wanted.'

And I said, 'Yes, but only ever for two seconds.'

And Franziska said that was for at least two seconds longer than I did, and then she stormed out.

'But I know exactly what I don't want,' I called after her, for instance I didn't want her to leave. But she didn't turn round again, didn't even stop in her tracks, I just saw her giving me the finger from behind and then she disappeared between the trees and I heard the car door slamming a moment later, heard her starting the engine, heard her driving off, and the tyres screeched so loudly at the corner that it sounded like a bad sign.

But I wanted a good sign; that much I knew. And I wanted Franziska to be wrong, I wanted her assessment to be absolutely incorrect and I wanted her to have to admit as much. She should be dumbfounded and apologize, tell me she'd really been wrong about me, and I'd nod and say, 'I guess you're right about that.'

I went to bed determinedly and the next morning I got up determinedly, went across to the house and sat down at the breakfast table with my grandfather. 'All right,' I said, and my grandfather hardly looked up from his newspaper, biting into his bread roll and chewing so slowly that my determination began to let up again.

'What's all right?' he asked in the end as he turned the page with a great rustle.

I took the newspaper out of his hands. 'All right, we'll go,' I said then, and waited for the relief to set in.

16 May, Beijing

My dears,

Beijing is absolutely beautiful but incredibly tiring. The noise is particularly exhausting—there's constant shouting everywhere, everything hooting and blaring and jingling and rattling. The traffic is beyond belief—cars, bicycles, mopeds, even donkeys crowding the streets. Grandfather and I don't talk much when we're out and about. 'Noisy here,' one of us shouts sometimes and then the other one shouts, 'Yes,' and then we quieten down again. Someone here has to be quiet, after all.

As you can imagine, I had put together a tightly regimented sightseeing programme for our three days in Beijing, but Grandfather proved so unenthusiastic about my plans that I struck most of it off the list. So today we went only to the Forbidden City. Grandfather strode through the three majestic large halls (Hall of Supreme Harmony, Hall of Middle Harmony, Hall of Marginal Harmony) with a bored look on his face (he called the emperor's throne 'flashy' and the Nine Dragon Screen 'implausible'). It was too cold for him in the Pavilion of One Thousand Autumns, and in the Hall of Mental Cultivation he claimed he had nothing to cultivate. But the clock exhibition did amaze him, although he couldn't resist asking the other visitors if they knew what the time was. There are huge clocks there in the shape of elephants, floating clocks in the shape of carp, tiny clocks in the shape of aphids. There are clocks that make a mechanical robot paint Chinese symbols with a little brush once every hour, which are supposed to be beautiful poems, there are clocks from which a golden rose grows until eight o'clock, blossoms until four o'clock and withers by midnight, there are clocks that go backwards and clocks that go sideways and clocks that don't go at all because they apparently stopped at the exact moment when Emperor Xianfeng died.

At some point Grandfather got tired. I deposited him in the Starbucks branch next to the Clock Exhibition Hall and viewed the rest of the Forbidden City on my own. When I went to pick him up afterwards he had disappeared. After a long search I finally found him in the Palace of Heavenly Male Clarity. He was sitting on a step with his eyes closed, two coffee cups alongside him and groups of tourists washing round him. When I nudged him he gave a cheerful wave and held one of the cups out to me. The coffee was stone cold but I drank it anyway, not wanting to disappoint him. We sat there until the palace was closed, swaying to and fro to dodge all the knees and bags, and sipped at our cups even long after they were empty. 'We really are in China,' Grandfather said on the way home.

'Probably,' I said.

It's now just after ten (so just after two in Germany). Grandfather's gone for a walk—he says the coffee's made him jittery. I've given up looking for an Internet cafe and have stayed behind on my own in the hotel and now I'm writing to you sitting on the bed because there's no space on the desk. Grandfather's put all sorts of photos of all of you on it. The untiring noise of Beijing is wafting in through the window.

Missing you and sending hugs,

K.

My grandfather had just looked up in surprise at the break-fast table. 'Of course we'll go,' he'd said and then had taken another bite of his roll, and I was appalled that my sudden assent was not properly appreciated, that he was obviously taking no notice of my determination. 'I'm sleeping with the woman you love,' I whispered, kept whispering it in the weeks that followed whenever something about him appalled me, even if it wasn't quite correct. But I didn't let that bother me because 'I've slept a couple of times with the woman you used to love until recently,' didn't have nearly the same effect.

'Pardon?' said my grandfather.

And I said, 'Nothing,' and then he started off with the possible travel routes, which he instantly recited by heart to me, mentioning countless names of towns, mountains, temples and restaurants, and I'd had enough of all that already so I interrupted him and said I'd prefer it to be a surprise, and then I got up and went back to the garden house. He certainly had managed to surprise me.

That afternoon I got my brothers and sisters to give me the travel money; I thanked them and they protested—'We're the ones who have to say thank you.' I didn't worry myself about how to pay my share; something would turn up. So far, something always had.

'I'm going to China,' I said on the phone the next day, and Franziska said that was new to her, and I said, 'It certainly is,' brand new in fact, and I hoped that Franziska's silence on the other end of the line was an astounded silence. But a few seconds later I heard her biting into an apple with a crunch. It seemed that everyone I talked to that day had to bite into something, it seemed that my determination was an incredible appetite stimulant, and then Franziska asked with her mouth full whether that was all I was calling to say, and because I didn't want to admit that was true, because I didn't want Franziska to take another bite of her apple or even hang up, I said, 'Of course not,' I had something important to say to her, and I hoped I could come up with something that might be important. She could hardly wait, Franziska told me, biting into her apple nonetheless, and perhaps it was her loud chewing, perhaps I wanted her to choke on it, or perhaps I just couldn't think of anything else, at any rate I said, 'I'm going to leave you,' and I was instantly annoyed at how recited it sounded. And Franziska didn't choke on her apple; all she did was give a contemptuous snort. Oh was I now, she said, and added that it was too late for that because if she recalled correctly she had left me the previous day, and I said she hadn't been particularly clear about that, had she, and anyway she'd done that so often before that I never knew when to take her seriously.

And Franziska said, 'Always,' I should always take her seriously, and I asked why she wasn't just consistent for once, and Franziska said she didn't want a lecture on consistency from me, after all I didn't even have to stand by my decisions because I never made any decisions, and she bit into her apple again with such a loud crunch that I had to move the receiver away from my ear.

And then I said, 'All right, we'll get married then,' and Franziska really did choke. How on earth did I get that idea, she asked once she'd finished coughing. 'Why me?' I said, it had been her idea in the first place. And Franziska thought for a moment and then seemed to remember what she'd shouted out of the car window, gave a brief laugh and said I must have got the wrong idea, she'd never suggested getting married, only that I make her a proposal, and I said that was typical of her, everyone had to make a big effort over her but she always refused to commit herself, and Franziska asked what I knew about big efforts, and I said, 'Plenty,' and told her not to keep changing the subject. 'Are we getting married or not?' I asked; in fact I yelled.

And Franziska yelled, 'All right, we'll get married.'

And then I yelled 'All right,' as well, and Franziska yelled it again.

And we battered each other with 'All right's for a few minutes until Franziska yelled, 'When?'

And I yelled back, 'Tomorrow.'

And Franziska yelled, 'Why not right now?'

And I yelled, 'OK then, fine.'

And then Franziska stopped yelling and said in a calm voice, 'OK, see you in a minute,' and hung up.

And I listened to the dialling tone for a while and then said quietly, 'All right,' and left the house.

Franziska got to the registry office before me, of course. Hands on hips, she was waiting for me outside the entrance. 'At long last,' she said as I came running up. She'd been wondering if she shouldn't have taken it seriously, she said.

And I said, 'Always. You should always take me seriously,' and I asked if we were there to have a chat or to get married, and Franziska suppressed a smile.

'Let's get it over with,' she said, and that was just what I wanted to do. I wanted to hurry now, I wanted to be fast enough for once, I wanted to get on with it quick-sharp because once we'd got on with it I'd be able to deal with it, or at least I hoped so.

But we couldn't get on with it. He couldn't do anything for us at such short notice, said the registrar; he didn't have a free spot for the next two weeks. 'May's very popular, you know,' and I was honestly appalled because the last thing I needed was time to think it over. I begged him, I insulted him, I even slipped him a banknote out of the envelope with our travel money in it, but it was of no use. None of it seemed to bother Franziska. 'What's two weeks anyway?' she asked.

And I said, 'Probably nothing for you.'

And then I realized I was supposed to be in China in two weeks' time, but I didn't want any new problems right then, I didn't want to postpone anything even more because the rush was doing me far too much good. All I wanted now was to say yes to everything, so I said it when the registrar asked, 'Then we'll put you down for the twenty-fifth of May?' and I said it when Franziska said, 'At least we're engaged now,' and I said it when she announced that we had to celebrate and later on I said it every time she asked, 'Another drink?' It was only right at the end of the night when I was in bed that I stopped saying it. Then I said no, and I said it quickly several times in a row, but it was too late by then and this time I wasn't sure I'd come up with a solution in time.

The casino had been Franziska's idea and I'd nodded to that too, of course. 'Come on, let's break the bank,' she'd said, and she told me she'd come up with a sure-fire system. 'All we do is put our money on twenty-five and five every time,' she whispered in my ear, because that was our wedding date after all, so she'd eat her hat if those numbers didn't come up.

And that made sense to me too, I'd have thought it was a good omen too, and I felt a need for good omens. And then when only other numbers came up to begin with—I remember nine, thirty-three, eighteen—I didn't worry. We hardly looked at the wheel, we were so busy discussing what to do with our winnings—our honeymoon, holiday homes, Pacific Islands. I remember twenty-one coming up, and two, and seventeen and eleven, and the two piles of chips that Franziska moved onto our squares grew higher and higher, and the one in front of us grew smaller and smaller. Thirty-one came up, three came up, I began to watch with a wary eye. 'Don't worry,' said Franziska, 'twenty-five's coming up now, I know it is,' and she pushed our remaining chips onto the layout, laughing at me in anticipation, even crouching and clenching her fists while the ball was still leaping wildly from number to number, so she could start cheering straight away.

But twenty-six came up and Franziska looked at me with such shock that I said a quick 'We're really close now.'

And although I didn't quite trust Franziska's sure-fire system any more, I took the envelope with the travel money out of my pocket and exchanged some of it for new chips. I just didn't want the evening to end like that, I wanted to exorcize the tiredness gradually coming over me, I wanted to cheer, I wanted to throw chips up in the air, I wanted to throw Franziska up in the air, I wanted to hand out ridiculous tips to the croupiers and buy a drink for everyone in the house so they'd raise their glasses with us, so they'd congratulate us, so at least we'd be getting on with things here. And zero came up, twelve came up, thirty came up, and I took even more notes out of the envelope, Franziska following it all with a slight sway and eyes already glazed over, thirty-five came up, seven came up, that goddamn eleven came up again, and it couldn't be true, twenty-two couldn't be true, nineteen couldn't be true, nor eight, but eight came up and I screwed up the envelope in my fist. I sobered up in seconds, the headache kicked in and so did the sour taste in my mouth. 'What a pity,' said Franziska, 'maybe it'll work out tomorrow,' and she ordered another cocktail that I didn't know how we'd pay for. Where were we going next, she asked me with a grin. Nowhere, I said, I was very tired, and Franziska pulled a face. This wasn't what she called a proper celebration, and I agreed with her for the last time that day.

The next morning I called my grandfather. I wanted to get it over with on the phone. There was nothing I could do, I said—'sadly'—all the flights were booked up and the earliest we could fly was in four weeks' time, although, of course, we couldn't because the money was all gone and it'd still be all gone in four weeks' time, and I was already annoyed with myself for not saying four months, for not saying half a year, not saying 'for an indefinite time', foot-and-mouth disease, contradictory entry conditions, warnings from the foreign office, now of all times, yes, I knew, I was very disappointed too.

My grandfather didn't seem to be disappointed at all though, and nor was he angry or upset. 'I can't go in four weeks' time,' was all he said, and he said it in such a neutral tone that I hoped the whole China thing was finally off the agenda and maybe we'd go away somewhere for two or three days, to the seaside perhaps, I could deal with that, I was almost looking forward to it. But then he said again, 'I can't go then, that's just too late,' we absolutely had to go earlier, he said, and I heard him pacing up and down. But that just wasn't possible, I was afraid, there just weren't any flights left. 'We'll take the car then,' he said, and I realized shockingly quickly that he meant it.

So I said as calmly as possible, 'You can't go to China by car,' but my grandfather was having none of it, of course you could, he told me, there wasn't a sea anywhere on the way and the journey wouldn't be all that long. 'Five thousand miles,' I said, 'as the crow flies.'

'There, you see,' said my grandfather, and I got the feeling I wouldn't be able to talk him out of the idea now.

'You're not allowed to drive,' I tried nevertheless, although that would probably be the least of his problems and he rarely abided by the ban anyway. My grandfather had never been a good driver; he needed a new car every few years because, of course, no insurance company would cover the cost of anything. Once he couldn't afford that any more he started driving never faster than twenty mph, soon not even hearing the other drivers constantly hooting their horns.

He wouldn't even crank up the speed on the autobahn. 'Why's everyone in such a rush all the time?' he'd ask as he crawled along on the hard shoulder, and the best thing to do was quickly reply that you didn't know either.

He'd never let anyone convince him to buy an automatic. They were for old people, he said. He preferred to take his only hand off the steering wheel every time he changed gears or to ask one of us grandchildren to hold it for a moment while he adjusted the mirror or undertook a long search for a new station on the radio. That meant at least one of us had to sit on the passenger seat even in our early years, even take my grandfather's place behind the wheel when he got tired on long journeys. He'd given us driving lessons as soon as our feet reached the pedals, in isolated supermarket car parks by night. 'It's just like riding a bike,' he told us, except you didn't have to be so careful with a car.

We liked the night-time driving lessons, no matter how tired we were, not yet realizing that my grandfather was intending to train for himself an entire fleet of chauffeurs. Now and then he'd call us from a pub at night, if he'd drunk too much even by his own assessment, and would make us take a taxi to the pub so we could take him and the car home safely, claiming he'd need it again in the morning. And, at the very latest, once we all had our official driving licences, apart from my younger sister, he almost never drove himself—at most to first dates, but even then it wasn't unknown for him to ask us to wait outside the restaurant in the car for a few hours. 'I owe you a favour,' he'd say, and he usually stayed in our debt.

So I was hardly surprised when he responded to my helpless attempt to dissuade him on the phone with 'You'll do the driving, of course.' I most certainly would not, I answered, and my grandfather said, 'Please.'

I'm not sure he'd ever asked me for anything before, aside from orders disguised as requests—'Could you please stop shouting,' 'Please don't ever ask me that again,' 'Please don't make a fool of me,'—but now he really did say 'please,' and all of a sudden there was nothing I could say in response.

'I'm sorry,' I said, probably a few too many times, before I hung up.

17 May, Beijing

My dears,

This morning Grandfather said he'd stay in bed, yesterday's food hadn't agreed with him (*huoguo*—a dish called hotpot, in which you cook the ingredients you order directly in the broth, classically lamb, cabbage, tofu, potatoes, snake or macaque). But I was not to worry about him and to have a nice day on my own.

I found it difficult to decide on a destination, everything in Beijing sounds so tempting—Garden of Perfection and Brightness, Garden of Ten Thousand Spring Seasons, Garden of Hundred Thousand Spring, Garden of Eternal Spring. There's the White Cloud Temple, the Azure Clouds Temple and the Cloud Dispelling Temple. I decided—partly due to the heat (it's over 85 degrees today)—on the Summer Palace, an immense park full of pavilions, temples, gardens and lakes. It also harbours the marble boat of Empress Cixi. It doesn't float, unfortunately, but that didn't bother the empress. She loved marble; everything had to be made of it. She ate tiny cakes covered in a paper-thin layer of marble off marble plates; she was carried around in a marble sedan chair, requiring twenty strong slaves, who also had to wear marble hats on their heads. She slept in a bed carved out of marble next to a marble husband equipped to the very last detail, whom Cixi even named the heir to the throne in her will, and who

really did officially rule the country for two days in the tur-
moil of the oncoming twentieth century.

In the afternoon I bought presents for all of you at the
western end of Liulichang Xijie—huge numbers of pirated
DVDs, a Chinese kite, a small talking Buddha (if I understood the saleswoman rightly, he says, 'The wise man waits
for the egg before he boils the hen') and a Rolex. You can
divide it up however you like between yourselves, and
before you complain don't forget what I went through for
your sakes. At least four vendors were constantly hassling
me, all holding identical jade sculptures under my nose in
one hand and a sword in the other hand—with me unable
to tell whether they wanted to sell me that too or threaten
me with it—and there were occasional duels between the
vendors, which were instantly surrounded by a crowd of
onlookers who started betting money on one or other of
the men. I made use of the tumult to escape every time.

In between, I tried to call Grandfather at the hotel but
he didn't answer the phone. Yet when I returned to our
room in the early evening he was sitting on the bed in his
shoes and coat (he always wears his coat despite the high
temperatures, probably so he doesn't have to admit there
was no need to bring it along). Where had I been for so
long, he asked, and then he told me we had to go out again
straight away so as not to be late. Grandfather had got us
tickets for the Tiandi Theatre. I was actually too tired and
hungry but Grandfather brushed my objections aside.
'Anyone who goes to China without seeing acrobats might
just as well have gone to the Westerwald,' he claimed, and
besides he'd already eaten. Not a word was said about that
morning's nausea. He was very excited in the taxi. He did

ask 'How was your day?' but he didn't listen to my stories, repeatedly looking at his watch instead. How much further must it be, he asked every few minutes of himself rather than me, seeing as I didn't know either.

We arrived just on time. I was too exhausted to follow the performance properly—there was lots of jumping, lots of stacking, rather too much twisting and turning for my liking, and everything was so fast and chaotic that even by the end I didn't know exactly how many acrobats were actually whirling about in their red costumes. There seemed to be at least forty of them, but perhaps there were only three.

Grandfather was absolutely transfixed. Contrary to his habit, he didn't make a single comment during the entire performance, not shouting out like the rest of the audience whenever the little boy was thrown a few yards through the air at a dizzying height, nor cheering with relief when the boy dangled safely from the arm of one of his fellow acrobats. He didn't react at all, not even during the final applause. After the finale he leapt up straight away and ran out, leaving me waiting for him outside the exit for almost half an hour. 'We can go,' he said then, and he seemed to be disappointed about something.

At the Donghuamen Night Market I ate a kebab while Grandfather drank a beer, in an evil mood. Did I know that Beijing would be buried by the Gobi Desert in a few years' time, he asked me. It was only a hundred and fifty-three kilometres away now and it was creeping closer by the day. It'd all be over here then, and he personally wouldn't shed a tear over the place. He had to stick out one more day here, I said, because our train to Xi'an didn't leave until the next night. Grandfather shook his head. 'What a waste of time,' he said.

He's sleeping now, restlessly and noisily. I'm sitting on the edge of the bed next to him and writing this letter. Rain has set in outside and it sounds as if it intends to stay for ever. No traffic noise for the first time, only the angry patter of the raindrops. I'm not tired at all any more.

Hope you're all well,

K.

Had we lost a lot of money yesterday, Franziska asked me that evening. She had come by unannounced and had lain down on the bed straight away, her voice still brittle, sunglasses concealing the top half of her face. 'It's all right,' I said, and Franziska nodded in relief.

'Good,' she said. She couldn't remember all that much of the evening and she'd been a bit worried. But she remembered the part with the wedding rightly, didn't she, she asked with a laugh, and I was tempted to shake my head in confusion, to ask, 'Wedding?' to ask, 'What on earth gave you that idea?' But if Franziska was reckoning on me taking it all back she had another think coming. I just nodded and joined in with her laughter, because something about it must be funny, I just didn't know exactly what that was.

We laughed for an unpleasantly long time, both of us presumably not wanting to stop because then we'd have to behave in some way, we'd have to behave in some way for the next two weeks, until the wedding, and even after that to be precise, but then at least we'd have got it over with and that would make it easier.

And because I had no idea how to behave, because I wished I could skip those two troublesome weeks, I said I was afraid I had no time, I urgently needed to start packing, and I began randomly throwing clothes in a pile. Franziska raised her head from the bed. 'Where are you going?' she asked.

'To China,' I said, I'd told her that, hadn't I, and her head dropped back onto the pillow.

'Of course,' she said and giggled, 'China,' and I asked what was so funny about that, I'd given my grandfather a vacation for his birthday after all.

'And I stand by my word,' I said as I folded shirts and trousers a second time because I was gradually running out of clothes that I could pretend I had to pack.

'That's good to know,' said Franziska, and now she thought she'd better get out of my way. She stood up, removed her sunglasses and blinked at me with small eyes. 'When are you leaving?' she asked.

'First thing tomorrow morning,' I said, and Franziska nodded and told me she'd thought as much.

I should get in touch as soon as I was back, she said then at the door, and I said, 'Of course I will,' and Franziska put her sunglasses back on, stroked my arm for a moment and then left. A few steps later she turned round again. 'Have a good trip,' she said. 'And say hello to your grandfather from me.' And that at least I'd really gladly have done.

I've rarely, probably even never, seen my grandfather as happy as he was during the year and a half when Franziska was my last grandmother. Even at her first time round to dinner, his eyes sparkled to and fro between her and us grandchildren. 'Isn't she great?' he asked when Franziska popped to the bathroom and we nodded honestly and not because this was the first time my grandfather had asked our opinion on one of his lady friends.

In the weeks that followed we saw him smiling almost uninterrupted. He was constantly telling us something Franziska had said, something Franziska had done, something he'd experienced with Franziska the previous evening or something he'd only just found out about himself through Franziska. He kept seeking physical contact with us during that time, stroking our hair, hugging us, massaging our necks, sometimes running his hands so devotedly over one of our thighs that we could only assume his mind was on another leg entirely.

He seemed to have decided to get closer to us on an emotional level too. 'Tell me, how are you actually?' he often asked out of the blue, assuming a look as confiding as he could muster. And if we answered fine or OK, he nodded in satisfaction. 'Lovely,' he said. 'That's really important to me.'

Wasn't it all getting a bit too much for them as well, I asked my brothers and sisters after a while, and they acted amazed. 'Why?' they asked. It was a delight to see him like that. 'Franziska just does him good,' they agreed unanimously.

The only thing we all wondered—except my grandfather himself—was what Franziska wanted with him, what she saw in him, what he had done to deserve her, to be honest. Because of course you could find my grandfather charming, you could even find him witty under certain circumstances, at times he was clever and, whether he liked it or not, experienced. And of course he looked astonishingly good for his age, he got everyone he met to confirm that, a lot of things about him were astonishing for his age, but his age itself was pretty astonishing too by that point and it was so far removed from Franziska's that questions arose automatically.

For that reason, we'd watched Franziska very closely in the beginning. We'd watched all the younger grandmothers and the explanation was usually clear enough. Franziska, however, displayed no conspicuous deformities and she neither spoke to angels like one of her predecessors nor only spoke Malay like another. She didn't radiate despair and we couldn't accuse her of any worrying complexes, and so nothing about her initially explained why on earth she was making do with a man so much older than her. The previous grandmothers had long since exhausted my grandfather's not particularly impressive fortune, so this time it wasn't down to that either.

It was only later, once I'd found out the little about Franziska's life that she chose to reveal, once I'd got to know the terrific verve with which she moved, with which she talked, her speed at shopping, at eating, in traffic, that I realized that Franziska was more than a few years ahead of her supposed age, that her advance got greater with every day. She lived at such high velocity that she must have caught up with my grandfather long ago.

At some point much later on, she once told me a little about her first marriage ('The first of how many?' I'd asked and got no answer). She was a teenager at the wedding and at the divorce too, and the formula with which she explained the split, usually so helplessly euphemistic—'We grew apart'—sounded plausible for once in her case, because from a certain speed it probably makes no difference whether you're moving in the same direction or in two different ones—the distance between you grows either way.

Not once, Franziska told me, not even at the end when it would have been a handy explanation to finish things, had my grandfather said he was too old for her. She could only remember one evening, quite early on in their time together, when my grandfather had looked at her for a long time and had said, 'If only we'd met thirty years earlier.' She'd been four back then, Franziska had pointed out, and my grandfather, she told me, had said, 'Then I'd have waited for thirty years.'

18 May, between Beijing and Xi'an

My dears,

I'm sitting in the dining car on the night train to Xi'an. With a great deal of luck we managed to get tickets for the hard sleepers, but Grandfather and I are sleeping in separate compartments. I visited him a while ago and he seems to be getting on marvellously with a young Chinese woman. If I saw rightly, he was reading her palm and she was giggling. He signalled that I was disturbing them so I came here to eat a bowl of noodles. In Chinese dining cars you have to take a number and you're not allowed to place your order until your number is displayed above the serving hatch. I've got number four hundred and eighty-nine and we've only got to one hundred and two, although there are only six other passengers in the restaurant car. It doesn't matter though, I've got plenty of time. The journey to Xi'an takes eleven and a half hours, my compartment is hot and muggy and there'll no doubt be snoring. But a smiling waiter brings tea quickly without even being asked. Every sip does me good, for today was another very strenuous day.

Grandfather had refused to look at any more of Beijing, so I booked an excursion to Badaling through the hotel, to view the Great Wall. It was still raining and Grandfather could only be persuaded to leave the bus after much effort. In an evil mood, he stood beneath the umbrella he'd borrowed from the bus driver, staring at the tourists in their brightly coloured raincoats, at the souvenir stalls covered by tarpaulins, at the rocking cable cars and the blurry hills. 'A majestic sight,' I said, not wanting to put up with Grandfather's disinterest any more, not wanting to admit he was right although it was actually a rather sobering sight. I too had imagined a construction that we thought for decades could be seen from the moon would be more impressive, but I wasn't going to let him see that. So I walked up and down, took random photos, bought far too many postcards and even patiently watched the epic information film, in which hordes of grubby Manchu warrior actors butcher a handful of freshly powdered Chinese soldier actors. Among other things, we were informed that the fires on the watch-towers were fed with wolves' droppings. 'Did you know that?' I asked Grandfather, hoping to get a word out of him at last.

'Yes,' he said.

On the way back the bus took a detour to a private clinic, supposedly a special service provided by the excursion company. We could be examined there free of charge by 'specialists in age-old Chinese medicine'. I suspected Grandfather would finally lose his temper but it was quite the opposite—he was suddenly all ears. 'If there's one thing the Chinese are good at it's getting old,' he explained.

The private clinic was a squat new building in the middle of an industrial estate. Half a dozen doctors or doctor actors were waiting at the door and waving. We had to line up to be examined one after another at astounding speed by the no longer waving but listening, tapping and feeling doctors. Grandfather put up with the long wait with awestruck fidgeting, his eyes wandering shyly round the bare examination hall from the neon strip lights to the diagrams, from the cacti in order of size on the windowsill to the plastic Buddha enthroned upon a small fountain in the middle of the room.

When it was finally Grandfather's turn, the doctor started by feeling his forehead and his little finger, pressed at several places on his thighs, belly and chest and took his pulse. 'A hundred years,' he said in German, patting Grandfather on the shoulder. 'With correct medicine,' he added. He wrote something on a piece of paper and handed it to the waiting nurse, who then disappeared into another room with Grandfather. It was my turn next and I was also felt in various places. The doctor spent a conspicuously long time on my earlobes before diagnosing 'Impotence,' then adding, 'sadly,' and writing something down again. Then I too was taken into the next room, which contained countless shelves full of mysteriously labelled phials behind a counter. The nurse handed me one of the phials, apparently at random, and demanded six hundred yuan. I refused politely, at which she asked if I didn't want to have any children. I already had enough, I answered, but she was having none of it, one could never have enough children and, she asked, how many poor girls and boys did I want to deny a happy life through my impotence. Her final offer was five hundred yuan, my family must be worth that much to me. I continued to refuse as she pressed the phial firmly into my hand. I was only half a man in my state, four hundred yuan and I could find a new, young wife and start a better family with her; thanks to the miraculous medicine I could get any woman I wanted. I had to go now, I was afraid, I told her, all my many children were getting impatient. 'Three hundred yuan,' she called after me. 'For the sake of mankind.'

Grandfather was waiting outside, clutching a couple of small phials in his hand. 'Real tiger's claws ground,' he whispered happily in my ear. 'You can't get it on the free market.'

When we left for the station earlier today, he seemed to have reconciled himself with Beijing. He insisted on pressing a generous tip on the hotel concierge to say goodbye, although I'd impressed upon him that tipping was seen as an insult here. An old adage even says that every tip accepted is revenged later by the loss of a tooth, and the concierge did hold his cheek in concern as he wished us a good journey.

A little later: I've since been able to order my noodles and they were prepared miraculously quickly. While I was eating, an older Chinese man sat down at my table. He gestured at the surrounding tables in apology, although all of them were vacant. For a while he watched me writing my letter to you, then he unwrapped a pair of chopsticks from a napkin and began helping himself to my noodles. When I looked at him in surprise he smiled, picked a piece of chicken out of my bowl and fed it to me. And so we ended the meal, him placing a bite into my mouth and his mouth by turns. When the bowl was empty he got up, said a few words I didn't understand as he gestured at the letter, then left the dining car. I feel very lonely all of a sudden.

Thinking of you all.

Best wishes,

K.

Franziska came by early that evening, or at least I was fairly sure it was Franziska. A succession of heavy, fast footsteps, then a knock at the door that set my pulse beating at exaggerated volume, so loud I was afraid it might be audible through the thin walls of the garden house. Another knock, then the footsteps started again, sounding out once round the house until they stopped only a few inches away from me. Franziska must have been standing right outside the window. I almost thought I could smell the leather of her boots. She was probably pressing her forehead against the windowpane and shielding her eyes with her hands, and I took a look round the room as well to be on the safe side. As far as I could see there was nothing in her range of vision to hint at my presence, and I was almost glad of the confirmation at last that my days under the desk fulfilled their purpose, but now I wanted Franziska to leave. What was there to look at for so long? She should be convinced by now that I really wasn't there.

And just as she took the first step away from the window the phone rang. 'It's me,' said the woman from the hospital, not giving her name. It was after six in the evening, so either she was working longer after all or she was calling me from home—which wouldn't have surprised me either. 'Where on earth are you?' she asked, no longer making any effort to be friendly. It really was urgent, she said, and I could come during the night if need be. Then there was a sucking sound, as if she was drinking something through a straw. 'I hope I can count on you,' she said and hung up, and I heard Franziska give a soft snort outside and her footsteps finally moved away, and I released my breath and was angry beyond all measure.

I was angry with the woman from the hospital, who was obviously incapable of identifying a body without assistance, who was apparently not at all worried about me although I'd been meant to leave the house ten hours ago. But I couldn't leave the house before I knew how to convincingly transport my grandfather from the Westerwald to China, or from China to the Westerwald. And I was angry at his thoughtlessness for dying so unconvincingly, I was angry at his thoughtlessness for dying at all, dying wasn't like him in the slightest. And I was angry with my brothers and sisters, who apparently had nothing better to do than keep looking out of the windows constantly, who spent hours lurking round the house so that I couldn't move freely. I was angry with China because it was simply much too far away, and I was angry with the Westerwald because it wasn't far away enough. Most of all, I was angry with Franziska, who kept calling me, who even just came round although I'd told her plainly enough I'd be going to China. She obviously didn't trust me, and how was I to marry a woman who didn't trust me, and I'd told her plainly enough that I'd get in touch as soon as I got back, and now getting back would be slightly delayed. What was so bad about that? Our appointment at the registry office wasn't until tomorrow afternoon after all, so there was plenty of time.

We'd never celebrated Christmas with any of my grandmothers. They always came along in springtime and left in autumn at the latest—late October, early November. Now and then one would stay until the first week of December, but they were exceptions. Some said goodbye to us, some stormed out of the house without a word, lots of them kept calling on the phone for weeks and we had to say my grandfather wasn't at home. 'Just tell her I'm dead,' he'd whisper from a safe distance.

So last autumn a farewell mood came over me about Franziska too. I began counting the weeks left for her, but then came December and she was still there, Christmas came, New Year came, and my brothers and sisters and I kept exchanging surprised looks whenever Franziska sat down at the breakfast table and said 'Good morning,' as if it were the most normal thing in the world. As spring passed those looks became rarer; we were getting used to Franziska. Perhaps my grandfather was finally settling down, we speculated. Perhaps he'd had enough of his dalliances, perhaps he'd finally finished sowing his wild oats and was ready for a responsible relationship. We got really drawn into these conjectures. There was talk of weddings, there was talk of family holidays, my elder sister even talked of a possible baby brother or sister, who would actually be a baby auntie or uncle, and then it all started again. We heard Franziska's car driving off more and more often at night, we put her unused plate back on the shelf more and more often after dinner, my grandfather sat motionless in his armchair more and more often, only his jaw slowly moving to and fro—it was all too familiar.

All too familiar were the words that echoed over to my room when Franziska and my grandfather argued at night—the familiar 'stubborn', the familiar 'pig-headed', the familiar 'ignoring me'; and of course it was only ever Franziska I could hear. Only the occasional mutter came from my grandfather, probably, but it might have been the water pipes gurgling.

We usually then heard Franziska stomping down the stairs in her boots and pacing round the living room at speed. 'I need a run,' she said to me once, having been so clearly audible that I'd gone downstairs to check she was all right. It was only much later that it occurred to me that I could have gone upstairs to my grandfather too, and I persuaded myself I knew he didn't want company in that kind of situation anyway.

I stood still in the middle of the room, only my head following Franziska as she walked round me in ever decreasing circles, taking sweeping strides with her hands on her hips. 'Is it my grandfather?' I asked, as if I hadn't heard a word of their argument.

'No,' she said. 'It's that idiot up there who looks just like him.'

After a few minutes Franziska's circles were so tight round me that I had to turn with her so as not to lose sight of her. She was getting faster and faster, beginning to run, I propelled myself only on tiptoes, the living room behind her began to blur, then Franziska blurred too, and when we finally lay on the floor, which was revolving in all directions, we ought to have laughed. But all we did was lie next to each other, breathing deeply, our eyes fixed on the ceiling as it gradually came to a standstill. Then we stood up, gave each other a brief nod and shook hands, still swaying slightly.

'All right now?' I asked.

'No,' said Franziska.

19 May, Xi'an

My dears,

Today was a very eventful day and I can hardly wait to tell you all about it. Now I'm sitting here in the Wenyuan Dajiudian, a large but nevertheless endearing three-star hotel convenient to the Muslim quarter. Its name, as the friendly concierge explained, means something like 'home of the intellectuals'. Apparently it originates from the 1950s, when illegal grasshopper fights took place in the back rooms, war-like duels in which not much money but a great deal of honour was at stake, very popular among artists and academics. To keep unwanted guests at bay, the fights were therefore announced as 'poetry readings'. It's almost midnight and this morning already seems unimaginably long ago.

It began with an argument. Xi'an, so I read somewhere, is a city you can either love or hate. Only minutes after our arrival, still in the taxi from the station, the parts were shared out between Grandfather and me—he took care of the hating and I was left with no other option but at least pretending to love this second stop on our journey. What Grandfather found too modern, I was forced to find contemporary, what Grandfather considered overcrowded I referred to as lively, he said dusty, I said earthy, he thought it ridiculous to spell a city with an apostrophe, I demanded far more apostrophes in city names, more semicolons, more quotation marks, more exclamation marks, and when Grandfather then said, after a period of sulky staring out of the window, 'A bell tower. My, how original,' I shouted at him. Why had he insisted on coming to China in the first place, why had he talked of nothing else, China here, China there, if now, now he'd got his own way, now that we really were in China, he was going to show no interest in the country, not show a trace of enthusiasm, react to all my suggestions with 'Is it very far away?', with 'I bet they don't have a toilet' or 'That's only for Buddhists.' What on earth had he expected of China, I asked him, and I asked very loudly, because he looked at the floor and said nothing at first, then shrugged and said quietly that he hadn't wanted to come to China all that badly as I was saying, it had just been a vague suggestion and he couldn't have known I'd leap upon it the instant he said it. And then he really did give me a conciliatory smile and said we were here now and we'd just have to make the best of it, and I said no, we didn't have to at all, if he asked me we could go straight back home again, right that minute. And I made expansive gestures at the taxi driver to take us back to the station. And Grandfather made even more expansive gestures at him to keep going straight on, even grabbing at the steering wheel from behind until the driver braked unexpectedly and gave us to understand that we were to leave his car immediately. So there we were in the middle of a four-lane highway, with hooting and shouting and complaining all round us. Grandfather didn't move a muscle, watching our taxi disappear in the traffic.

'There's something I've got to do here,' he said calmly.

And I asked, 'Right here? In the middle of the road?' and he looked at me.

'No,' he said, 'here in China,' and then he cut his way across to the hard shoulder, taking no notice of the braking cars. I followed him with our suitcases.

'And what, if you don't mind me asking?' I asked him.

'Something personal,' he said and marched determinedly towards the city centre. I didn't even try to keep up with him.

Something personal. As if I'd thought he had urgent business matters to deal with here, as if I'd thought he'd responded to an official invitation. By the time we arrived at our hotel an hour and a half later I had decided to agree with him. It really was our only option to make the best of it all, and the best option seemed to me to ignore Grandfather as best as I could. In the hotel room I lay down on the bed and switched on the TV, while Grandfather fastidiously tidied his shirts and trousers into the wardrobe just like every time we get somewhere, even though we only wanted to stay one night. He even has various ties with him, putting one on in the morning every now and then, looking at himself in the mirror for a long time and then deciding against it after all.

There are a striking number of shows on Chinese TV about oral hygiene. Three different channels were showing close-ups of people brushing their teeth, some of them in slow motion, accompanied by an expert who repeated their motions on a plastic model of a jaw.

Grandfather enquired what the plans for the day were and I pretended to be absolutely riveted by the TV show. When he kept asking me things I even took my toothbrush out of my luggage and followed the on-screen instructions.

Grandfather stood by our bed for a while longer, unde-
cided, and then left the room. I carried on brushing my
teeth. I must have done it for a very long time because the
next show or the one after that was on by the time Grandfather came back, a bowl of soup in his hand. 'Maybe
you're hungry,' he said. I removed the toothbrush from my
mouth and his eyes proudly followed every spoonful I
ate—was it good, he asked several times, the soup wasn't
too hot, was it, he could get me some salt if I needed it.
When I'd eaten he stared into the empty bowl. He'd
allowed himself to purchase two bus tickets to see the Terracotta Army in Bingmayong, he said, and he told me he'd
be delighted and honoured if I were to accompany him.
And although I wasn't sure whether he only wanted to
make up with me because he was bored or because he
really was sorry, I consented. I'd found out more than
enough about oral hygiene.

In Bingmayong we hired a guide for fifty yuan, who
at least spoke English. I had to translate everything into
German for Grandfather, although he claimed it wasn't
necessary, constantly nodding at the guide's explanations
and saying 'Ah yes,' at inappropriate moments.

The Terracotta Army really is impressively large. It
consists not only of thousands of warriors, armed to the
teeth with swords, spears, crossbows, dagger-axes and
pitchforks, but also of countless horses, wagons, chariots,
catapults and even a whole column of dogs. According to
the guide they really did exist in the army of Emperor Qin
Shi Huangdi, whose grave the terracotta warriors are
guarding, although the canine ranks broke up in cowardly
fashion only minutes into their first battle.

Before the age of forty, this Qin Shi Huangdi had already conquered six important kingdoms, the guide told us, which Grandfather made him confirm several times but then brushed aside—who needed that many kingdoms, for goodness' sake!

Towards the end of the tour we came to the large hall in which over six thousand soldiers are lined up and, truly, not one of their faces resembles another's. Some look determined, some afraid, some are laughing and some seem to be asleep, some have a slight squint and some are sticking out their tongues. We could count ourselves lucky, the guide said at the end, for they say the army comes to life every two thousand two hundred and seventeen years, and today of all days was that date. Grandfather flinched, the guide gave a leisurely laugh, said, 'Just a little joke,' and vanished on the spot, leaving Grandfather and me alone among the stone warriors.

Of course we were lost only a few steps later. Endless rows of soldiers extended in all directions and still seemed to be giving Grandfather the creeps. He stopped a few times and stared one of them in the face—'He just winked, I could swear he did.' At some point he was too exhausted to take any further notice though. He needed a break, he said, and we took a rest on one of the horse-drawn chariots.

I tried to get my bearings from there, but no matter where I looked all I saw was a mocking gaze out of terra-cotta eyes. I did find it a little exaggerated, I said after a while, to have an entire army guarding you when you're dead, but Grandfather didn't agree at all. 'If I ever died I'd do just the same,' he said. You never did know, did you?

I started getting nervous too, not so much at the idea of the warriors coming to life (although I had to admit that I'd already thought about making the most of the riders' probable initial sleepiness to jump on one of their horses and make a dash for the exit—presuming the horses came to life as well, that is), but more out of fear of stumbling about there until the excavation site closed. A hungry night with a frightened Grandfather was not what I called 'making the best of things'.

Did he happen to have anything to eat with him, I asked Grandfather. He searched his coat pockets but found only a couple of sticky boiled sweets that he always helps himself to at hotel receptions. 'Two each,' he said proudly, then thought about it, looked at me for a long time and said, 'You know what, you can have three.'

Before I could thank him, we heard voices and followed the sound and came across a group of Spanish tourists whose guide had apparently also just made the little joke about the two thousand two hundred and seventeen years—a few of the Spaniards were looking round fearfully and the guide was giving a leisurely laugh. In the end he showed us to the exit for twenty-five yuan extra.

I bought Grandfather a miniature warrior in the gift shop. 'Just one to start off with,' I said, but Grandfather seemed to find even that little warrior unsettling, and he threw it into a bin when he thought I wasn't looking.

We said nothing at all for most of the journey back, and it was only once we'd reached the outskirts of Xi'an that Grandfather suddenly asked me what would have happened if we hadn't come across the Spanish tourists. I told him we'd surely have found the exit at some point. 'But what if we hadn't?' he asked.

I didn't know quite what he was getting at. 'Then we'd probably have died of thirst,' I said. Grandfather nodded a few times. Perhaps they wouldn't have found our corpses for years, he said, and something about that idea seemed to appeal to him. I considered that highly unlikely, I told him, and Grandfather shrugged; it was too late for that anyway, he said.

This evening he insisted on going to the circus again. I had no idea that he loved acrobatics so much, I said, and Grandfather said there were lots of things I didn't know about him, and I didn't contradict him.

This time I let him go alone, though, which didn't seem to bother him. I was glad to have a quiet night in and I'd just got caught up in a dental-care documentary (evening shows seem to be filmed with a studio audience, who laugh surprisingly frequently and sometimes even shout and scream), when Grandfather appeared again. Hadn't the performance been any good, I asked him. 'Oh, no, it was good,' said Grandfather, 'but it wasn't right for me.'

Instead we took a stroll round Xi'an. This time we didn't run the risk of getting lost, because the city is pleasantly linear despite its size. Drawn up like a chessboard, the streets form squares in which the shutters on the houses are painted black and white on alternate blocks.

In Xi'an too, the city is at least as busy at night as by day, with children frolicking on the streets and dozens of people waiting outside many restaurants in orderly queues. As soon as the waiter calls out that a table is free, however, the queues are transformed into a seething mass and violent confrontations are not uncommon.

So Grandfather and I only got tea from one of the many improvised street stalls and knelt down on the pavement, as everyone seems to do here. A few children eyed us suspiciously at first but then dared to come closer, even touching Grandfather's nose gingerly and then climbing all over him, which he put up with.

'Thank you for coming with me,' he said to me then.

'Of course,' I said, and that it had seemed to be very important to him to come here.

Grandfather brushed a child's hand off his face and said, 'Yes,' but he wasn't quite sure any more what he actually wanted here.

We drank our tea and watched the comings and goings on the street. A group of businessmen in suits sped past us, loudly ringing the bells on their tandems, an old woman sat cross-legged on the bonnet of a moving Jeep doing her embroidery, while a whole family were getting their hair cut on the opposite pavement, all of them ending up with the exact same hairstyle and looking very pleased.

Grandfather smiled. 'Lian always used to say I'd like it in China.'

Who was Lian, I asked, and Grandfather cleared his throat. 'I guess I've never told you about her,' he said. The children were still clambering about on him, a small boy playing with his empty dangling shirtsleeve, a girl trying to plait his thinned hair. 'Lian was the strongest woman in the world and my one true love,' Grandfather said, and it sounded like he'd been looking forward to saying those words for a very long time.

As usual, I didn't take it all too seriously when Grandfather mentioned love, especially true love, but this time something seemed to be different. He didn't say it in a voice of pride in his ability for intense emotions, he didn't even sound nostalgic, it was more of an incontestable fact of which he was informing me, something that was easy to check, something written in every school book.

Had I ever met her, I asked, but Grandfather shook his head. 'It was all a very long time ago,' he said. 'I was just as old as you are now.' I tried to imagine Grandfather at my age. For some reason he had a thin moustache and a cap pulled down over his forehead in a sprightly style, a toothpick in the left corner of his mouth and his gaze was stiff and shy, his arms so tightly folded that I couldn't make out how many he had.

'Lian came from China,' said Grandfather. 'Her name means something like "graceful willow" and I couldn't imagine a name less suited to her.'

Were we here to look for her, I asked, but Grandfather shook his head, oh no, she'd been dead for years now. 'I just want to know if anything here reminds me of her,' he said.

I waited for Grandfather to tell me more but all he did was stare silently at his tea. The children had fallen asleep at his feet. He was tired too, he said, and we went back to the hotel.

Now I'm lying here writing all this down for you and I can't stop thinking about Lian. Have any of you ever heard Grandfather talking about her? Why has he suddenly started? Perhaps he just made her up, because there's one thing he's right about—there really is a lot I don't know about him.

There's so much I don't know about all of you either. Perhaps next time we should all come to China together.

I send hugs to you all.

K.

Since that first incident in the living room, I met Franziska there after every row she had with my grandfather. Luckily enough, there were plenty of them, and I started feeling pleased when the mood was so tense over dinner that it was only a matter of hours. If the worst came to the worst I helped things along by apparently unthinkingly mentioning some tricky subject or other, by playing loud music late at night, by disseminating a little false information. After a while Franziska was walking her circles round me almost on a daily basis, even after relatively calm evenings, and I began to hope she was deliberately starting the odd fight so as to seek refuge in the living room as often as possible. And there I'd be waiting for her.

It was during these very weeks that my grandfather's body began its decline, comparatively slowly at first. That still had an increasingly strong adverse effect on his mood, which meant I hardly had to help out any more. Just to be on the safe side, I occasionally made a few of his tablets disappear or slipped up with the spices in his portion of dinner.

To begin with, my grandfather battled against his unfamiliar fragility. He started renovating the garden house with his one hand, he signed himself and Franziska up for a tango course (although they left the first class early for reasons unknown to me and never went back) and once I even saw him holding one of my younger sister's earrings up to his bare chest in front of the bathroom mirror, as if trying it on.

On Franziska and his anniversary, only three months ago now, he took her out one last time. 'Don't wait up,' he'd said to us, most likely as a boast rather than to spare us unnecessary worries. And in fact it was two o'clock in the morning when my telephone rang. Franziska spoke so quickly I could barely understand her but I made out the words 'ventricular fibrillation' rather frequently, so frequently that I repeated them to myself all the way to the hospital and I couldn't even stop at the information desk. Was I all right, I was asked a number of times, and I said I didn't quite know yet.

My grandfather was already in the operating theatre, as it transpired. How did it look for him, I asked in the emergency room, and the nurse attempted a smile. 'Don't you worry,' she said, nudging me towards the waiting area, and I tried to follow her advice as best I could, even though she hadn't told me why not to worry.

Franziska was sitting in the furthest row of hard plastic seats in the waiting area, a crossword puzzle resting on her crossed legs. As I came closer I saw that she was busy painstakingly shading every single space. She didn't look up at me until she'd finished the very last one.

'He promised me he won't die,' she said, and it sounded like that information was intended to pacify me. I nodded and sat down next to her. Franziska was wearing her blue raincoat with not much underneath, as I now noticed. When she saw me looking she pulled down her coat tails and held onto them.

I ought to have called my brothers and sisters, of course, but then they'd inevitably have all come immediately and my second-eldest brother would have wanted to speak to the consultant, my elder sister would have cried, my eldest brother would have said what was most important was keeping calm, he'd have said it very often and very loudly, and my younger sister would have been offended— it was just typical of my grandfather, she had an exam in maths or biology or English tomorrow and she had no time for ventricular fibrillation right now.

So I said to Franziska, 'Let's go for a walk,' and Franziska put the crossword aside, reached for her handbag and then looked at me.

'I can't move my legs,' she said, and to prove it she lifted her dangling thigh up with both hands and dropped it again.

Next to the coffee machine was a folded-up wheelchair, into which I lifted Franziska. 'Giddyup,' she said, and I pushed her along the abandoned corridors into the entrance hall, past the display cabinets of old-fashioned obstetrics instruments—forceps and hooks and straps that you could guess at the use of without wanting to find out anything more detailed—and out into the grounds. I hadn't noticed the cold on the way to the hospital, isolated white spots in the flowerbeds, frost or late snow. 'Faster,' said Franziska during our first circuit, 'Even faster,' during the second, and on the third circuit she had to grip the armrests with both hands, the tiniest bump throwing her up in the air. Sooner or later I'd stumble, there was no doubt about that, and I'd let go of the wheelchair when I did, but I had the feeling that was just what Franziska was hoping for. Her coat tails had been blown aside and her bare legs, still crossed, bobbed up and down. 'Faster, faster,' called Franziska. I was gasping so loudly I could barely hear her, the cold air stinging my lungs and my eyes burning, and I saw Franziska take her hands off the armrests and then I let go.

The sudden lack of resistance made me fall forwards. I hit the frozen ground, rolled over onto my side and came to a standstill on my back a few rotations later, bare branches swaying above me. The pain was pleasantly clear, in my shoulder, in my jaw, in my elbow, in my knee, the taste of blood, the crunch of gravel or splinters of tooth or both. Someone laughed and I wondered for a moment if it was I.

The wheelchair was lying sideways in a flowerbed, one wheel still turning. A few yards alongside it, Franziska had already sat up. Her raincoat was torn and she had blood on her chin and knees. She beamed at me. 'Come on, let's go and visit him,' she said, and I had to think for a moment who she meant. Still swaying, Franziska stood up and held out a hand to me.

'You can walk again,' I said.

'Yes,' she said, 'it's a bloody miracle.'

The emergency-room nurse gave us a brief sceptical gaze but didn't ask any questions. 'He's asleep now,' she said, and it was only my relief that made me realize how badly prepared I'd have been for anything else. There was no one in sight at the ward. We waited a few minutes and then began searching for the right room door by door. We found him behind the fourth one, motionless on his back, tubes in his arm and nose, as one might expect. For a while I watched the reassuringly unchanging numbers on the ECG while Franziska closed the door behind me.

We didn't dare go too close. A strip of light fell through a gap between the curtains onto his face, which showed no expression whatsoever, not even exhaustion. For the first time, I thought he looked old, even older than he really was, as if he ought to be in a glass case.

The second bed in the double room wasn't occupied. Franziska and I sat down on the tightly stretched bed linen, our legs hardly touching the floor. Like obedient children, we looked over at my grandfather as if he'd ordered us here, and didn't say a word. The grazes on my knees and elbows began to throb and the blood on Franziska's legs was almost dry now, a small trickle ending somewhere in the middle of her calf. She removed it with spit, then felt all her other wounds, on the ball of her left hand, on her right upper arm, on her temple, and then she turned to me, her eyes leaping about my face and stopping at my chin. She touched it cautiously with her thumb and a stinging pain immediately made me flinch. My skin was obviously grazed there too without me having noticed. Franziska did not pull her thumb away though and the stinging increased, became a throbbing, a burning and finally a soothingly widespread pain. Franziska's gaze remained fixed on my chin, not even moving while she undid my trousers with her other hand, and with a few speedy moves she'd undone my belt, my buttons, and I was embarrassed at how clearly welcome her hand was, so clearly that Franziska left it at a brief check and got up, not taking off her raincoat, pulled down her underpants, squatted over me and, still removing neither her eyes nor her thumb from my chin, slowly lowered herself onto me. Her arousal showed fewer signs than mine; for a few tormenting seconds almost her entire weight pressed upon a single point, until at last she came closer to me, inch by inch. I saw her biting down on her lips in pain and I too clawed firmly into the bedcover to stop crying out. We hardly had to move, we felt every tiny clench, every thrust of our circulation instantly. Her left hand still didn't leave my grazed chin and with her right hand she first supported herself on my knee and then, when we did begin to move, grasped my neck so that my head was jammed between her left hand and the inside of her right arm and I had a direct view of my grandfather over her shoulder, although that was the last thing I wanted to see. I willed myself to close my eyes but I just couldn't, I saw his age-spotted arm, I saw his sunken chest, the obtuse angle of his jawbone, Franziska moved faster, her right hand clawed into my shoulder, I saw one of his bushy eyebrows, I saw the shallow flicker of the side of his nose, I saw him opening his eyes, Franziska pressed me deeper and deeper into her, my chin throbbed under her thumb, I saw my grandfather blink a few times, look down at himself and then turn, our eyes met unprotected, I still couldn't move my head, I still couldn't close my eyes, Franziska buried her hand in my hair, my grandfather's stare attached itself firmly and then I came.

I must have closed my eyes for a moment after all, for when I opened them my grandfather's were definitely closed, his head was still on one side and the numbers on the ECG were unchanged too. I checked that right away.

20 May, Luoyang

My dears,

We got up very early this morning to see a bit more of Xi'an before we left for Luoyang. I wonder whether it was a mistake to pack our itinerary so tightly that we can only spend a short time in each place. Like in Beijing, we left Xi'an with the flat feeling of not having seen nearly everything. But as you can't ever see everything anyway it seemed to make more sense to visit as many different things as possible, and it didn't seem to bother Grandfather either. He still gets bored easily and it's usually I who ask him to walk a little slower.

He was very interested in the Temple of the Eight Immortals to begin with but then he was visibly disappointed that none of them was present in person. We spent longer in the History Museum. It's always surprising which things were common in China much earlier than in Europe. One of the murals is an extremely detailed picture of a polo match, a kind of brochure from the Tang dynasty made of thin tissue paper shows illustrations of cosmetic surgery, albeit rather rudimentary, and one of the small clay figures from the Sui dynasty is definitely wearing a tank top.

Unfortunately, we didn't have time to go out to the Famen Temple, where Buddha's four finger bones are kept, the second-oldest relic after his right big toe in Puning Temple.

Instead, we went to see the city's two most important landmarks, the Big Wild Goose Pagoda and the Heron Statue, both dating back to the seventh century when Taoism went through a brief ornithological period.

For lunch we had cold noodles in peanut sauce, apparently a regional speciality but Grandfather refused to believe that. He made the waiter warm it up and shouted after him, 'Next thing you know, the stains on the table-cloth will be a regional speciality.' I ate the noodles cold.

The train to Luoyang took five hours. Grandfather read a Chinese newspaper he'd bought at the station—'I'm bound to get the gist of it'—and I flicked through a travel guide and then looked out of the window, outside which gently wooded hills swayed past, between them huge rice paddies and rural settlements, which seemed to come from a different time with their bamboo huts and mules and farmers' wives in brightly embroidered aprons.

I wanted to find out more about Lian from Grandfather, although I was afraid he'd got the subject over and done with, that he'd barely look up from his newspaper if I asked a question, that he'd say, 'You and your Lian,' only to murmur a monosyllabic answer.

How had they met in the first place, he and Lian, I asked nevertheless, and Grandfather looked at me, then folded up his newspaper thoughtfully and put it down next to him. 'Are you really interested?' he asked, and I nodded vigorously. Grandfather smiled. It was all such a long time ago that I'd have to forgive him if he didn't remember everything very precisely.

He'd been a young man back then, at any rate, in the prime of life, he had so much energy and so many talents he'd wanted to try out everything, so he was constantly on the lookout for new activities. And so late one summer, he couldn't remember what year it was, he ended up as a magician in the then famous variety show Tamtam. As I knew, he could do a number of most astounding tricks, which had soon made him one of the main attractions at the Tamtam.

'You don't mean the shoelace trick?' I asked incredulously and Grandfather seemed offended.

'Among others,' he said.

I couldn't believe my ears—the shoelace trick! Do you remember how Grandfather used to perform it at every birthday party? It didn't usually work, and then Grandfather would shout, 'Who wants more sausages?'

'Anyway,' Grandfather continued. It had been a wonderful time at the Tamtam; he hadn't earned much but he didn't need much, and the ladies treated him well in those days too, he'd switched beds up to four times a night, but his heart—he looked at me earnestly—his heart had been as untouched as his own pillow in the morning.

It had been common practice at the Tamtam, he told me, to rent out the theatre to travelling circuses every now and then and so it was that a troupe of Chinese performers were their guests that year. At that time, Grandfather emphasized, China was highly exotic and they had expected large takings because lots of people would come to the shows simply to see real live Chinese people in the flesh.

It had been the middle of the night, said Grandfather, when the troupe arrived. He'd been woken in his little room above the theatre to help unload their caravans, although there was little to unload. The acrobats travelled light—a trapeze, a hoop, a tightrope; the sword swallower needed only his sword, the escape artist his chains. It was only when it came to the last caravan that they'd all been gathered together. It contained a large number of weights, and even the smallest of them was almost impossible to lift. It took ten men to carry the largest weight, even that only with the greatest of effort. Who on earth was going to lift those weights, Grandfather had asked one of the Chinese helpers during a breather, and the man had been amazed that Grandfather didn't know. 'They belong to Lian,' the awestruck helper said in surprisingly good German, 'the Massif of Macau.' Those chunks of iron were as light as soybeans for her. And why, Grandfather had asked, couldn't this Lian see to the transport herself, and the helper looked round in shock. Lian was a celebrity, a miracle of nature, and she needed her sleep right now.

Grandfather told the story with such verve that even the Chinese passengers on the seats round us stopped chattering to listen in. Now and then, when it seemed appropriate, they laughed out loud or sighed in sympathy. Grandfather looked round with a satisfied expression, got someone to bring him another drink and went on.

He was to see Lian in the flesh for the first time the next day. 'It wasn't love at first sight,' he said, anything else would be a lie, but he'd realized from the very first second that no other woman would ever measure up to Lian.

When he entered the variety theatre that afternoon, Grandfather told us, everyone had been terribly busy, attaching ropes, marking out positions, drilling and sawing and hammering, the acrobats limbering up in the foyer, the tightrope walker balancing on the balustrade in the gallery, the sword swallower working up an appetite with a few daggers in the dressing room. Only Lian was doing nothing, enthroned motionless on a divan in the courtyard of the Tamtam, a slice of pineapple over each eye, a young Chinese man fanning her, another massaging her shoulders with a kind of wooden paddle, a third placing spoonfuls of ice cream into her mouth. Never before, said Grandfather, had he laid eyes on a woman of such magnitude. He'd been rooted to the spot, incapable of removing his eyes from her intense corporeality, from her immense number of chins, from the bulging flaps of skin that hung tightly packed along her arms and legs, and least of all from her little finger, which came creeping out of the meatball of her hand like a glutted maggot.

The young Chinese man massaging Lian's neck had noticed him after a while and chased him away with a torrent of words and swings of the paddle, and it was only when Grandfather thought himself out of harm's way in the foyer that he'd noticed he had an erection.

He didn't take in much of the evening's performance because he was waiting for Lian's act, which was at the end of course, being the highlight of the show. After the troupe's director had announced a 'world sensation' in many words, most of them incomprehensible, the cart holding Lian's weights was pulled onto the stage by four of the most muscular acrobats, with much moaning and groaning. To prove that the weights weren't a cheap trick, Master Hu invited more and more men from the audience up to the front to lift the weights off the cart. In the end there were twelve of them, and their faces were all dripping with sweat.

Then the lights dimmed, only a single spotlight directed at the weights. No one in the auditorium dared take a breath, least of all Grandfather. 'I knew my life was about to change in a single second,' he said. 'I didn't know if it would be for the better or the worse, I didn't know if I wanted it or not, all I knew was that I wouldn't be able to do a thing about it.'

And then came Lian, her boundless body swathed in a sparkling gold cloak, her long hair plaited round her head, her eyelids shaded black, her face powdered white, a painted moustache swingeing from one cheek to the other.

With tiny steps, she scampered to the weights, bent down to the smallest of them—which had only been lifted by two men from the audience together—hoisted it aloft with her right hand, tossed it in the air, caught it with her left hand, twirled it a little between two fingers and then dropped it to the floor again without a sound. The audience cheered; Grandfather smiled an enchanted smile.

And so it went from one weight to the next. Some Lian lifted with her teeth, some she held between the folds of her belly for seconds, some she balanced above her head with such levity that it looked as if the weight were pulling her upwards, and Lian did all this with an air of indifference, almost boredom, which Grandfather didn't know whether to find sinister or disreputable. 'I looked her in the eye all the way through,' he said, 'and I felt like I was looking into a well, so deep that you wouldn't hear a stone landing at the bottom, not even a boulder.' The people round us on the train all started laughing at the same time again but fell silent the instant they noticed Grandfather's confused look.

It was only at the last weight, he said, that he'd seen something akin to tension on Lian's face, and perhaps it wasn't just a dramatic contrivance that she needed three attempts to get the weight above her head. She took a few steps forwards and backwards and then she had her balance, and while the audience was applauding frenetically, two acrobats dropped down onto either end of the weight from above, then more and more leapt to join them until in the end the entire troupe formed a pyramid on the iron bar. As the cheers went on and on, Lian first lifted her left leg off the floor, then let go of the dumb-bell with her right hand and threw kisses towards the hollering auditorium.

He could still see her now, Grandfather told us, the veins on her forehead so swollen that they were clearly visible even through all her fat, the sweat leaving streaks down her powdered skin, her whole body quaking and surging so strongly that he could feel the draught even in the fifth row.

'Never before and never since have I seen anything as beautiful,' he said. 'I was absolutely happy and at the same time utterly devastated, because I knew that from then on I would not rest until I had managed to win over this woman.'

It was just at that moment that we arrived in Luoyang. Our Chinese fellow passengers all pressed their business cards into Grandfather's hand and said long, complicated farewells. 'What pleasant people,' said Grandfather as we got off the train.

We knew from the travel guide that Luoyang wouldn't be an attractive city. Like most tourists, we'd come for the famous Longmen Grottoes, which we want to see tomorrow morning. The square outside the station was bustling with ducks and geese, but otherwise the city is very quiet. The people here walk much more slowly than in Beijing or Xi'an, almost creeping round. Drivers hoot rarely and almost shyly, and there's hardly any shouting. There's a layer of melancholy above Luoyang, perhaps because this former metropolis (which was the capital for sixteen and a half dynasties) has never quite returned to its former glory since its devastation in the twelfth century. They really do take their time over things here.

We're staying at the Shenjian Hotel, which is supposed to be close to the station. But there are no recognizable house numbers in Luoyang (the reason being—so we were told—a delivery delay dating back to the Tang dynasty) and the hotel doesn't have an English sign, so it took us almost an hour to find it. Along the way we tried to ask passersby for directions, but they eyed the characters in our travel guide with such sad looks that Grandfather gave them pitying pats on the back.

We had dinner at the Zhen Bu Tong Fandian, the famous water banquet. It consists of twenty-four courses, in which no ingredient may be used twice. The banquet used to be held literally on the water—diners hired a kind of raft and a rowing waiter transported them to the various courses simmering away on small islands. The only reminder of all that today is a small water-lily pond in the middle of the restaurant, in which the traditional feast is represented by lovingly painted plastic figures.

Although the separate courses aren't very large, I still took only a few bites of the last five. Grandfather, however, seemed rather disappointed. He had been counting, he made me explain to the waiter, and there had only been twenty-three dishes. He stuck to his guns for so long that they eventually brought him a bowl of rice, which he hardly touched, however. It was 'slightly inferior in quality,' he said.

I kept trying to steer the conversation onto the subject of Lian during the banquet. How had he got to know her in the end, I asked not long after the tenth course. He prodded the fork he still insisted upon into something we could only hope was some kind of mushroom, then gingerly topped up our teacups before saying, 'I was the one who had to tell her she didn't have much longer to live.'

During the day Lian had always been completely shielded off. Two ferocious-looking guards had stood outside the corridor to the courtyard, usually not reacting at all to Grandfather's entreaties to pay his respects to the artiste, or sometimes reacting with laughter. Grandfather, however, as he told me, had still spent all day outside the corridor, in the hope of casting a brief glance at the huge object of his desire or at least hearing her voice a single time, but all he could make out was a slurping sound, sometimes sighing and occasionally a long drawn-out high tone, a kind of squeaking, 'like from a very small animal'.

Night after night he sat in the audience with a thudding heart and admired Lian's strength and beauty, day after day he spied and listened past the severe guards. He noted with concern that the slurping grew quieter and quieter over these days while the squeaking, on the other hand, got longer and longer, sometimes lasting several hours, and at some point the guards began to exchange worried glances too. Was everything all right with Lian, Grandfather asked, but they didn't understand him, and even if they had they couldn't have told him anything. They stared right through him, even when he started badgering them, even when he shouted that Lian must be sick and they had to let him through to her, even when he drummed on their chests with his fists. It was pointless, and after a week in which the squeaking graduated to a whimpering, Grandfather left his post outside the corridor to the courtyard, hurried into town, fetched a doctor, woke the director from his nap and persuaded him with words, gestures, shouts and threats to let the doctor examine Lian.

Grandfather himself had to wait at a distance. He spent half an hour pacing to and fro, and then between the guards he saw the doctor lead the director and one of the menservants, who was obviously acting as an interpreter, into a corner of the yard. The doctor spoke to them in a serious and resolute manner. He heard him ask over and over, 'Do you understand?' He heard 'heart', he heard 'liver', he heard 'kidneys', he heard 'everything really', he heard 'sadly', he heard 'two weeks', he heard 'at the most'. He saw the bewildered director shaking his head, gasping for breath, shouting at the doctor, then finally collapsing in tears and having to be carried back to his caravan by the two guards. Grandfather took instant advantage to step into the yard. Lian was lying on her divan, her eyes closed, her breasts, which overlapped her belly like two flatfish, heaving up and down but her body otherwise at rest. The servants who usually fed, massaged and fanned her had all withdrawn with the shock. His 'contradictory emotions',

Grandfather said as the waiter brought us new bowls, had taken his breath away at that moment. His almost painful delight at finally getting close to Lian struggled within him with his despair at what he had just heard. 'I gazed upon one about to die,' said Grandfather, 'and there was nothing I could do but smile.' And then Lian had opened her eyes and once again Grandfather had felt as if he were looking into a well, even deeper than the one he had seen on stage. The shaft seemed to go down for miles, and at the very end something was shining. There'd been a kind of reddish gleam and the longer he stared at it, the brighter it became, and then all of a sudden it had shot to the fore, all the way along the entire well shaft, straight out of her pupils and directly at Grandfather. For almost a minute, he said, he'd been blinded, and when he regained his vision at last, Lian had been staring unwaveringly at him and had said something in a quiet but firm voice. Naturally enough, he didn't understand it so he could only give an apologetic shrug, and Lian repeated the same sentence over and over, getting loud and impatient, and Grandfather wrung his hands because he so wished he could understand. And out of pure despair—Lian now sweating and trembling all over— he finally reached for the bucket of ice cream and began to feed her. Her trembling died down spoon by spoon and once the bucket was empty she took her hand and stroked Grandfather's cheek. And even though lifting weights every evening meant that every inch of her fingers was covered in a thick layer of calluses, he had never felt anything comparable to those few seconds.

Then she pulled her hand away and buried it in her lap, and Grandfather understood that as a sign to leave Lian in peace. He stood up but she held him back with a hoarse sound, barely audible; yet it made Grandfather freeze in his tracks. Lian looked at him, enquiring and fearful, and Grandfather attempted a smile, which he didn't quite manage, however, and Lian's eyes went on asking, over and over, more and more imploring, until Grandfather finally gave a sad nod, just a single time but it sufficed. Her gaze grew instantly vacant and she lay there absolutely motionless, so still that Grandfather feared she wouldn't even be granted two weeks. His breath faltered, something sharp stabbed at his chest, something large pressed at his throat, something wet ran down his cheek, halted a moment at his chin and then dripped to the ground, and Lian reached out her hand with a speed one would never have imagined her capable of, caught the teardrop on her index finger as it fell and dropped it into her own eye.

Then she said something else, once again in a very quiet, very purring voice. It sounded like thanks and farewell, and Grandfather took a bow, stumbled back to his room and spent the remaining hours before the performance attempting to process what he had just experienced.

As you can imagine, he took in even less of that evening's performance than usual. It was not just he who seemed to be worried whether Lian would come on stage at all; the audience was full of nervous whispering and the acrobats seemed far from focused during their act. Yet the director came on stage as usual after the tightrope walker to announce the 'world sensation Lian'. He was still visibly weakened but showed no other signs, although Grandfather thought he saw him swallowing a few times before mentioning her name.

Lian was wearing a red cloak that evening, her hair loose and coming almost down to her knees, the painted moustache turning up so far at the sides that it looked as if she were smiling. 'And perhaps,' said Grandfather, 'it didn't just look like it.' This time she lifted the weights with breathtaking ease, not even pulling a face during the finale with the pyramid, and when she stretched one leg in the air as a final flourish one might even have thought she had to try very hard to keep the other leg on the ground. She threw more kisses than usual, one for everyone in the audience, only hesitating when she came to Grandfather, drumming her fingers on her puckered lips for a few seconds, and then she slipped one of them into her mouth and winked at my Grandfather. 'That was the last time I ever blushed in my life,' he said, piercing a prawn with his fork and examining it for a long time before he put it back into the bowl.

After our sumptuous dinner we decided to walk back to the hotel. Our route took us through the deserted old town centre and the night market, where Grandfather ate a small snack (*dousha gao*—a sweet cake made from peas, dates and sugared beef), past the Wenfeng Pagoda, which has a pedicure salon on its top floor, and countless sex shops to the main square. And there, surrounded by brightly lit office blocks, we came across hundreds of people dancing. There was no music to be heard, no one seemed to be conducting them, and yet they moved in neat lines, absolutely synchronized in a complicated choreography. After Grandfather and I had watched this spectacle for about a quarter of an hour, the dancers began to clap all together, again with no recognizable cue, each embracing the one next to them. There were a few minutes of loud laughing and talking and then the square emptied out at lightning speed, leaving Grandfather and me alone. What on earth was that, I asked. 'A party,' said Grandfather, 'and we weren't invited.'

I think he sometimes feels slightly out of place here in China and perhaps he's homesick too. Today he put the family photo we gave him on his bedside table again, and he often wakes me in the night to ask me who the hell has secretly rearranged the room. I'm glad I've finally got an idea of what made him so keen to come, even though I still don't know exactly what he's looking for.

Tomorrow I'll try and send off all my previous letters at last. I hope you're all well and I look forward to seeing you.

All my love,

K.

First thing in the morning after the night in my grandfather's hospital room, I'd moved into the half-renovated garden house. I'd successfully evaded my brothers' and sisters' questions, and my grandfather hardly asked any when he'd been sent home a week later. 'Have you got everything you need?' was all he wanted to know, and I decided all he meant was the fixtures and fittings in the garden house, and nodded. My grandfather asked few questions from then on anyway, and gave few answers too, deteriorating before our very eyes at breakneck speed, his symptoms multiplying by the hour, and the only person who didn't seem to be worried about him was Franziska, even though she was the one who knew all about speed.

She had come round to see me on the evening my grandfather was discharged. 'Who does he think he is?' she asked, trying to pace up and down in the garden house, which was too small for that, however, so she jumped up and down on the spot. 'Does he think he'll find someone better? Does he think he'll find someone younger?' If anyone was going to do the leaving round here it should have been her leaving him, exactly, that was the right way. And she began randomly destroying objects—she picked up her wine glass from the table, twisted it a little and then shattered it with a sober blow against the windowsill, she cut neat zigzags into the net curtain with a pair of scissors, she threw my phone on the floor and stomped on it so thoroughly with the heel of her boot that it got stuck.

I was upset about my things but I still didn't try to stop Franziska. It did me good to hear the splintering, the cracking and the tearing, and I even held out suitable items in invitation—crockery, my bedside lamp, a ceramic ashtray. But she ignored it all and instead kicked at a chair leg until it broke off. Then she seemed to have had enough. She sat down on the bed and covered her face with her hands— but I didn't want her to stop now, I wanted her to smash the whole house to smithereens, I didn't want her to sit there all collapsed like that, and so I picked up the ashtray myself and threw it on the floor. It didn't shatter. All it did was slither two feet towards the bed and then stop somewhere between Franziska and me. We both looked at it. It was very quiet now.

'Shall I help you tidy up?' she asked in the end. I shook my head and Franziska got up. 'See you tomorrow then,' she said, as if that were the most normal thing in the world.

But I said 'See you tomorrow,' too, and I noticed that it made me happy.

Did she actually think he'd seen us, I asked Franziska when she was standing in the doorway. She looked at me blankly. 'Doing what?' she asked.

'You know,' I said, 'at the hospital.'

And Franziska frowned, and then she smiled for a moment and said, 'You wish.'

And I didn't know if I really did wish. I didn't know what would be worse—if he'd seen us or if I was only imagining it. And perhaps he had seen us but now he thought he'd imagined it himself, because he never mentioned that night to me—there wasn't even the tiniest hint—and all the changes in his behaviour towards me went unnoticed because so much had changed at once. Only once, as we were standing in front of the fridge together a few days after he came home, did he ask me why I hadn't visited him in hospital. 'I had a lot to do,' I said quickly, and he seemed to take my point.

'I could have died though,' he did say, however, and for the first time he said it without the dramatic tremor in his voice that usually accompanied everything he said about death.

I tried to smile. 'Not you, oh no,' I said.

Over the next few weeks Franziska came to visit me every couple of days, usually knocking in the middle of the night and starting to complain about my grandfather before she even got through the door. She complained that he made my brothers and sisters say he wasn't at home on the phone, even though she could hear him snorting in the background. She complained that his snorting had always driven her crazy, and the way he kept shuffling his feet at the dinner table, kept nodding his head, kept blowing his nose. 'That man can't sit still for five minutes at a time,' she exclaimed, and I nodded. I nodded at everything she said about my grandfather in the hope of her exhausting the subject faster that way, but she didn't exhaust it; my grandfather came bubbling out of Franziska non-stop—the movements he made, the things he said, the way he looked, the clothes he wore. And I waited, nodding my head, for Franziska to get more and more heated, and once she'd got heated enough she couldn't stay put in the garden house any longer, she had to go outside, she absolutely had to go over to the house to get worked up over there about everything and anything—the mess, the furniture, the supposedly impractically high banisters. On tiptoes and complaining quietly, she'd lead me up to my grandfather's bedroom, she'd imitate his snoring, which we could hear almost down the stairs, she'd even open the door to convince herself that he really was on her side of the bed, as she'd suspected, and she'd crawl into his room on all fours and eye my grandfather's facial expression disparagingly, the book on the bedside table, the dentures in the glass, and then usually she'd gesture me over, pull my shirt hastily over my head, undo my trousers, and then we'd sleep with each other.

It always went very quickly. We'd hold each other's mouths closed, neither of us letting my grandfather out of our sight. Now and then his snoring would halt and we'd freeze for a moment until it grew regular again. He never woke up, as far as I know.

Afterwards we rushed back to the garden house. Franziska didn't get worked up about anything after that, in fact she usually went to sleep immediately while I lay awake next to her for a while and didn't know whether the chaos was increasing or decreasing.

We never slept with each other outside my grandfather's bedroom, although I tried everything. I put photos of him by my bed, I taped his snoring and played it back at appropriate moments, I offered to let Franziska tie one arm behind my back. 'Why would you do a thing like that?' she asked, looking at me as if she'd rather not know the answer.

21 May, Shanghai

My dears,

I'm writing to you from Shanghai, which wasn't actually planned. I didn't arrive until late at night and I was still so furious at Grandfather that I booked myself into a single room. I didn't knock at his door and I can only hope he's worrying about me. It's now almost four in the morning. I'm sitting in the still busy hotel bar and drinking my third gin and tonic, or in fact my fifth if you include the two on the plane, and it won't be the last, that's for sure, after this absolute failure of a day.

It started with me waking up far too early this morning in Luoyang, perhaps due to the now unfamiliar quiet—no traffic, no spontaneous market outside the hotel window, no unasked-for cleaning ladies vacuuming the room while we were still in bed. Stupidly enough, I decided to leave Grandfather to sleep and set out in search of a post office so that I could finally send off my letters to you. They couldn't really help me at the reception desk. The porter did give me a map and pointed at a spot marked by a pigeon, but according to the key that was a public swimming bath and, as I found out after an unnecessary walk, it really was a public swimming bath.

In response to my enquiry at the tourist information centre they had to make several phone calls, involving an astounding amount of laughter. In the end, however, they gave me an address so far out of town that it wasn't on my

hotel map. They wished me good luck and it sounded genuine, so I jettisoned the note with the bus connections and
took a taxi.

The post office was hopelessly overcrowded, despite
the early hour. It would appear that Chinese post offices
are responsible for a large number of services—some customers were posting letters or parcels, but some were pay-
ing their electricity or water bills, some were renewing
their passports and some were having their pets vaccinated,
if I saw correctly.

I finally got to the front of the queue after three-
quarters of an hour. I presented my letters, pointed at the
words Air Mail, which I'd written in large letters below the
address, and just to be on the safe side I imitated a plane
with my arms. The postmistress watched me unmoved,
then opened the envelopes with a practised swish of her
index finger, took out the letters and held them up to the
light. One word—I think it was 'toothpick'—seemed to be
of particular interest. She called two of her colleagues over,
who leant over the letters with her, pointing at other words
and whispering, and then all three of them beamed at me,
shook my hand at some length and patted me on the back.
One of them even handed the customer behind me his
phone so she could take a photo of us shaking hands. Then
they all said something very ceremonious-sounding to me,
one after another. The postmistress stuffed the sheets
back into the envelopes, placed a carefully selected ink
stamp on each of them, and then handed me the envelopes
and turned to the next customer without further ado. I
searched in vain for another counter or a box for me to put
the letters into, then stood around helplessly for a while

and tried to divert the postmistress' attention back to me by waving the envelopes with a quizzical look on my face. Yet every trace of her previous effervescent friendliness had vanished. Not even looking at me, she rebuked me with a long stream of words. The next customer shoved me roughly aside and even her dog, from whose head she was just unwinding a large bandage, gave a threatening growl. As the waiting customers shook their heads in disapproval I left the post office. It had started to rain outside but there was no taxi to be had and so I walked in any old direction, not caring if it was the right one. When a flock of ducks came waddling towards me at a crossroads I drew back my leg to kick one of them up into the air but I missed it and the ducks quacked at me angrily. I quacked angrily back at them.

China is more stressful than you want to admit. At first the unfamiliarity is fascinating, then it gets tiring, and soon you start longing for things like horse chestnuts, junction boxes, baby buggies—all the things they don't have here. You want to be able to say 'Sorry,' you want to say 'No, the next one along,' you want to know your way round and understand street signs and block out other people's conversations because you instantly hear that they're talking about nothing. You can't block anything out here, it all makes an impression. And as I took random turnings in the hope of getting somewhere, I decided to change our itinerary, to cross off one stop or other along the way, perhaps even to persuade Grandfather to go to the coast for a few days, to a tourist hotel where there's nothing to take care of—full board, international cuisine, water gymnastics. I needed a break from China.

When I got to the hotel around midday, soaked to the skin, I was afraid I'd come back to a worried and reproachful Grandfather. But he'd already left. There was a plane ticket on my pillow and next to it a note saying he was afraid he hadn't been able to wait for me, he was on his way to Shanghai and would explain everything when I got there. 'See you this evening, have a good trip,' it said, and below that he'd noted down the address of a hotel and, apparently as an apology of sorts for his hasty departure, kept one of the peonies from the vase next to the TV on the pillow. I put it back in the vase, got into bed and tried to sleep. I wanted to sleep for days, I wanted to leave Grandfather to wander the streets of Shanghai alone, I wanted to leave him to wander the whole of China alone, I wanted him to try in vain to make himself understood wherever he went, I wanted him to be tricked and cheated in tourist traps, then mugged and robbed so that he wouldn't leave his hotel room out of fear and regret at having been so stubborn. I couldn't sleep, of course. I started worrying, of course. And I knew I'd take the flight in the end, of course.

It didn't leave until the evening so I had plenty of time to see the Longmen Grottoes, to give the detour to Luoyang some kind of point and also in the hope of raving about them to Grandfather later and telling him what a unique attraction he'd missed.

Unfortunately, though, the caves were a disappointment, which was possibly related to my bad mood. I'd just had enough of Buddhas, and no matter what cave I went into I found them smiling at me gently with their swollen lips from every nook and cranny, waving at me shyly with their right hands like someone who's not sure you remember them. And I'd had enough of the guides' droning voices—Wei dynasty, Sui dynasty, Tang dynasty, Hong dynasty; century after century tumbled over one another and I didn't care about them in the slightest. One of the caves was for worshipping ancestors, of course, another one had medical prescriptions carved into the walls, of course, and, of course, there were plenty of monkeys' eyes, snakes' teeth, pandas' claws, dragons' eggs and lotus flowers, lotus flowers and more lotus flowers. A third cave was dedicated to wisdom, but not just one wisdom of course, not ten, twenty or a hundred wisdoms—they had to have ten thousand of them, there has to be at least ten thousand of everything in China, nothing else is worth the bother. Ten thousand is apparently the smallest number they have here.

So I skipped the Extended Youth Cave and went to have a little lie down on the bank of the River Yi but I found no peace there either. First I was surrounded by another flock of ducks, and the way they tried to bite my leg made me suspect it was the same flock I'd come across earlier. And once I'd finally got rid of the ducks they were instantly replaced by Chinese schoolchildren, who left my leg alone but all wanted their photos taken with me. Two girls whispered something into my ear and ran away giggling and a group of boys wanted to buy my trousers. I demanded ten thousand yuan and headed back to the bus stop as they were still discussing the price.

My plane was almost two hours delayed, which hardly surprised me on a day like today. I was given a voucher, which, as I later found out, was only valid in a pedicure salon, so I had my toenails filed while watching a TV show about a man who stuck ping-pong balls up his nose.

I've just ordered one last gin and tonic, then I ought to be drunk enough to sleep. I'm very upset with you for not coming with us. I'm very upset with you for leaving me alone with him, just like you've always left me alone with him. I'd rather he'd neglected me too, believe you me, I'd rather see him as just an old man too. When I get back I'm going to move out of the garden house and get a proper flat, maybe even in another town, and I won't take anything with me, I won't call often and when I come to visit I'll be terribly friendly. You can count on that.

K.

I must have slept for a few hours at some point, because it was light by the time the telephone woke me. The woman from the hospital sounded indignant. 'You appear to be terribly busy,' she said, making the word 'terribly' longer than necessary. 'So busy that you don't even have time to make a short call.' Then she seemed to be slurping something again. 'Whatever the case,' she said—and there was a low bubbling sound—'I'm expecting you at some point today.' If not, she remarked, there were other methods of getting me there; she had plenty of other tricks up her sleeve. 'And don't forget the passport,' she added before she hung up.

Franziska called right after that and she was indignant as well, of course. She couldn't believe it, she said, the line had been engaged a minute ago. 'Was it that woman from yesterday? The one who was expecting you during the night?' she asked, followed by a commendatory whistle, and wondered if that was where I'd been all this time. 'Whatever the case,' she said then—and she said it in exactly the same way as the woman from the hospital—I was sure to know what day today was and she just wanted to ask without any obligation whether I'd perhaps manage to turn up, and if not she'd have a quick flick through her address book to ask if anyone else had time, it'd be such a shame to let the appointment go to waste when she'd taken the day off especially, and then the answering machine beeped, the number jumped one along, and a few seconds later the phone rang again. 'It's me again,' said Franziska.

'I just wanted to remind you about your ID card, you mustn't forget that of course. A tie's not that important.'

And, all of a sudden, I'd had enough of being reminded to bring identity papers, and I got up so suddenly that I bumped my head on the underside of the desk. I'd had enough of looking for explanations too, I wanted to have it easy now, I wanted to just nod again. Yes, I'd remember my ID card, yes, I'd bring my grandfather's passport, yes, I'd take the train to the Westerwald, I'd identify him, I'd arrange everything that needed arranging, and yes, I'd be back on time at three o'clock. It was all perfectly doable, I'd marry Franziska, and yes, I'd tell my brothers and sisters everything, even more than necessary, and yes, I'd apologize, I'd pay their money back. That would take a while, but it didn't matter because all of a sudden nothing would be urgent any more.

And up till then I'd just nod my agreement with everything, step by step.

So the first thing I had to do was find my grandfather's passport, and that meant I'd have to sneak into the house, like it or not. I dialled the number that had been my number until three months ago. It rang for a long time and then I set out.

In the winter I'd been able to see the house out of my window but now the leaves on the apple trees hid it almost entirely from view. Nonetheless, I'd got into the habit of leaving the garden house only through the window on the side facing away from the house. That meant I landed directly on a small path, at the corner of which I checked that the coast was clear outside the house, and I kept looking round after that until I reached the front garden gate.

I hadn't been there for seventeen days; it felt like much longer. And of course the house hadn't got smaller, that's not possible, and it must have always had so few windows. The only new thing was a sticker on the front door with a picture of an Alsatian and the words 'Dog on Guard'. As far as I knew that was a bald-faced lie.

I rang the bell by the gate, several times over to be on the safe side, although I didn't know quite what I'd say if someone did come to the door, and then I opened the gate, walked up the four steps to the front door and went in. The remains of breakfast were still on the dining table, along with those of earlier meals, it appeared. A small swarm of fruit flies hovered above the plates like a miniature mobile, an early wasp floating in the orange juice.

There had always been a permanent buzzing all over the house, a humming and crawling and creeping. In the summer we'd stretched tightly meshed nets across the windows but that was of little use. There was always a gap to creep through somewhere, there was always a light bulb to confuse with the moon somewhere, there were constant short sizzling sounds followed by a few seconds' silence. We were never allowed to take action ourselves, however. My grandfather had placed the invaders under his personal protection—'They're my poor, confused creatures,' he'd say. He wouldn't even hold a mosquito responsible when it settled on his arm to suck his blood. 'I've got plenty, I can spare a few drops.'

And the one time I managed to squash a fly with my hand, over lunch, I got an instant clip round the ear from him. 'What did it ever do to you?' he asked me over and over, and I cried and held my cheek and said it had annoyed me, that's what. 'No one gets squashed to death for being annoying round here,' exclaimed my grandfather, and he covered the dead fly with a box of nicotine chewing gum.

It appeared that my grandfather hadn't felt quite comfortable leaving my brothers and sisters unsupervised for so long. There were yellow notes stuck all over the house with instructions and warnings. 'Keep it short!' it said on the telephone; 'How about a cup of tea?' on the coffee machine; and on the bathroom mirror I found 'You're even better looking the right way round.'

I'd never seen so much looking after on my grandfather's part. The whole house was a mass of bright yellow. Some objects—the iron, the remote control, the birds' nesting box on the patio—he'd provided with so many instructions that they were barely recognizable beneath them. Even in the fridge, as I discovered to my astonishment, every product had its own sticker, on which my grandfather had noted down the best-before date already stated on the packaging, only in larger letters. Most of the dates were now in the past.

The house was in a state of neglect altogether. In the kitchen, crumbs and scraps of packaging had been swept into small heaps but not cleared away and a huge rubbish bag was overflowing with used coffee filters and yogurt pots. In the bathroom, the empty toilet rolls had piled up and the basin was smeary with grime, and I found used cups, cereal bowls, apple cores, randomly abandoned envelopes and odd socks in all sorts of surprising places.

It had never been really tidy in the house in any case. About once a year, usually just before the inaugural visit of a new grandmother, my grandfather would gather us up and distribute jobs. It'd take no time at all if everyone joined in, he'd tell us, but he was always the first one to retire to a comfy chair, usually only minutes later—'for a quick breather'—and he never complained when we grandchildren followed his example.

We'd even had a cleaning lady for a while. Three weeks later she was our grandmother; not a particularly long-term one, but my grandfather still never got a new cleaning lady.

I ought to have been in a rush. Time was of the essence after all—perhaps one of my brothers and sisters had forgotten something or might come home early, and apart from that I absolutely had to catch the next train so as to get back on time for three o'clock. But something or other put me in a daze, something made me look into every single room first, made me read all the little yellow notes ('This goes nicely with your brown trousers'—'Read something decent for a change'—'Not working at the moment'), something kept me away from the library though if the passport was anywhere in the house then it'd be there. The library was what we called the loft extension, although it hardly lived up to its name. There were in fact books there, piled up on the floor, and furniture like almost everywhere else in the house, but the room's main use was as a place to put everything we wanted to get rid of (garden chairs, fossil collection), everything that was broken (record player, airbed), outdated (typewriter, chest expander) and bizarre (antlers, trampoline), things that would one day be mementoes (attempts at pottery, my second-eldest brother's table tennis cup) and things still waiting to be used (cross-country skis, wok).

My grandfather used the library as a study although other, far less cluttered rooms would have been more suitable. Nevertheless, it meant that we grandchildren were officially not allowed in. Apart from the bathrooms, the library was the only room in the house that could be locked from inside. 'Everyone needs a bit of privacy,' said my grandfather, 'I don't just walk into your bedrooms, do I?' That wasn't quite true—he did always knock but never waited for any kind of 'Come in,' and often enough cigarette butts on the windowsills testified to him having prowled round our rooms while we were out. Now and again he quoted long chunks from my younger sister's diary verbatim, until she locked it away. But the decorative locks on our desk drawers were no real hindrance for my grandfather anyway.

'As usual: no entry,' it said on the yellow sticky note on the library door, followed by three of my grandfather's wedge-shaped exclamation marks, and I really did hesitate, as if he'd have minded now. We'd rarely abided by the no-entry ruling in the first place. The five of us had regularly sneaked into the library when my grandfather was out of the house, and although one of us always stood guard by the window, we only dared to whisper in there and jumped at the slightest sound. Yet, as exciting as it was to enter the forbidden room, we were disappointed every time by how few mysteries it housed. We'd expected so much more of the antique bureau, supposedly a family heirloom and, as the large number of ashtrays distributed round it suggested, my grandfather's workplace. Countless little drawers and cubby-holes would have provided space for numerous secrets but all they revealed was paperclips and coins, batteries, business cards and stray buttons. The desk surface would be piled up with papers, newspaper clippings with no recognizable theme, bank statements, receipts and business correspondence.

Only twice did we discover anything out of the ordinary. Our first find was a list, in which my grandfather had allocated a particular animal to all our names, in the closest he could get to neat handwriting. 'Keith: weasel', it said for instance, next to my younger sister's name he'd written 'seahorse', and next to my eldest brother 'stag beetle'. My grandfather had included himself in the list too: 'I: hamster'.

We weren't quite sure what these zoological comments were meant to signify but of course we didn't dare ask our grandfather. To our mutual horror, my second-eldest brother announced over dinner that he wanted a hamster for Christmas. My grandfather showed no conspicuous reaction. 'I'm not having one of those in my house,' was all he said, before he went on eating impassively.

I had forgotten the list until years later, when I came across it again on another rummage round the library. The 'weasel' after my name had been crossed out. It now said 'also hamster', and although I attempted to interpret the fact that I now belonged to the same species as my grandfather as a privilege, the redefinition came across as rather resigned.

I still couldn't bring myself to enter the library. I'd never been in there on my own, and I wondered for a moment whether I shouldn't change the order round and call my brothers and sisters first so we could go in together. I promised myself I'd ignore the list if I came across it; I didn't want to know what animal my grandfather had made me into by now, or whether I was still an animal and not a geranium, a pebble, a tiny piece of plankton. What I wanted to know almost less than that was what my grandfather had written after his own name now. After all that had happened in the meantime, I could hardly imagine he was still a hamster.

I once asked Franziska whether she thought my grandfather and I were similar. I wasn't sure what I wanted to hear, and she apparently wasn't either. She looked at me for somewhat too long before she said, 'Not a bit.' 'Really,' she added and smiled, presumably involuntarily, in an encouraging way.

All I used to do when my grandfather told me how much I reminded him of himself was nod, because most of the things he said we had in common were based on mere conjecture anyway. 'I've never cared what other people think either,' 'I didn't like raspberry ice cream either, you'll get over it,' 'I used to dream of going to sea at your age too,'—although I'd never wished for any such thing, and nor did it seem likely that my grandfather had either. In fact much of what my grandfather told us about his youth sounded exaggerated, romanticized or as if looted from other people's lives. And so we grandchildren took a sceptical approach to the second unusual thing we found in the library—a folder labelled 'Autobiography'. But instead of a lifetime's confession or a pot pourri of dubious heroic deeds, the folder contained only a single sheet of sparingly typed notes.

'Part one, chapter one,' below that several beginnings, all of which broke off after a few lines, sometimes only a few words or letters.

'It was raining on the day of my birth,' it said, for example. 'To sum up, I can say that', it said, 'Spr', it said, and between them were several attempts to describe a specific scene, apparently from his early childhood. 'A meadow. I must have been naked,' 'A meadow in summer, I walk nude,' 'A summer meadow. I am naked. My penis sways to and fro,' 'Meadow, summer, I don't know.' And then the manuscript broke off.

I had to get to the station in less than an hour's time if I was going to manage everything, so I yanked the yellow note off the library door, took a deep breath and walked in.

The room seemed to have got more cluttered. I spotted the no longer rocking rocking chair from the living room, the abandoned fish tank, and next to the window a whole collection of barbecue sets still in their original packaging. The bureau stood out all the more amid all the chaos. Even from the doorway I could tell the desk had been totally cleared, obviously even dusted—it had a veritable sheen to it and I hardly dared to touch it. Everything had vanished—the papers, the bank statements, the letters, I couldn't see any newspaper articles, no guarantee certificates, let alone the list of animal names and the aborted autobiography. It came as no surprise that the drawers had been cleared out too, with the exception of a single overlooked paperclip, which I gazed at for a while as if it might give me some kind of clue, and then returned it to its drawer.

The waste-paper bin was empty; I checked. I checked the piles of books, I pushed the unused furniture aside, I even took down the pictures from the walls but it was all to no avail.

I sat down on the no longer rocking rocking chair and tried to come up with a reassuring explanation for the disappearance of all the documents. Perhaps my grandfather had intended to sell the bureau and had to empty it out, perhaps he'd put the papers in a bank deposit box months ago, perhaps particularly neat thieves had been at work—but none of it seemed likely, I had to admit. I wasn't going to find his passport anywhere; he'd taken care of that.

Back downstairs, I cleared away the dishes and did the washing up, I cleaned the floor and took out the rubbish. I wasn't sure whether I was hoping for my brothers and sisters to come home. 'Keith, aren't you in China?' they'd ask.

And I'd say, 'No, as you can see, I'm not in China.' Where was Grandfather, they'd ask, looking round for him, and I'd say, 'Grandfather's dead,' and I envisaged my brothers and sisters staring at me in horror, having to sit down, wiping tears from their eyes and asking what had happened, and me saying, 'I have no idea. I really have no idea.' Hadn't I been with him, I imagined them saying, and I saw myself shaking my head. 'I lost sight of him at some point,' I'd say then, because that was exactly what had happened and because it might be exactly what my grandfather had wanted.

As I'd feared, the jam jar on top of the fridge was almost empty. I removed the remaining notes and a few of the larger coins; it might be just enough for my train ticket. As always, I was determined to memorize the amount I'd taken out—although I'd lost track of the total of my secret loans long ago. I'd once kept a list, next to every borrowed sum an insult or petty slight for which the money was supposed to compensate me. 'Because I had to play table tennis facing the sun,' 'Because my birthday's the last in the year,' 'Because I've got a cold,' 'Because I have to live in this family.' And though I'd given up the list years ago, I still always came up with an appropriate justification every time. This time was easy enough—'Because I have to identify the body.' The compensation was much too small a sum in fact, an absolute bargain.

The wad of yellow sticky notes was on the table next to the coat rack. My grandfather's last warning had pressed through to the top sheet, too faint to read, but I still plucked off the note and put it in my pocket.

My hand on the door handle, I turned round one last time and wondered whether my grandfather had turned round as well, to make quite sure he hadn't forgotten anything. I went back to the coat rack and wrote on one of the yellow notes, in an imitation of my grandfather's effortful block capitals, 'This is for all of you,' which I stuck to the frame of the picture of galloping horses. Then I left the house.

22 May, just outside Shanghai

My dears,

I'm sitting on the cramped back seat of a pickup and we've just crossed the city limits out of Shanghai. The itinerary I worked out is obsolete but that doesn't matter now. Grandfather's on the passenger seat. He's almost certainly too excited to sleep, and next to him, at the wheel, is Dai.

Dai was the reason Grandfather wanted to come to Shanghai so suddenly, and it's down to Dai that we're leaving the city so soon again now.

But let me start at the beginning. A few hours after I fell into bed last night, Grandfather knocked at my door for so long that I eventually let him in. He hadn't been worrying about me, of course, he didn't apologize for his hectic departure, he didn't ask how my day had been nor why I'd booked into a single room. All he did was beam broadly at me, exclaiming, 'We're this close!' and holding his thumb and forefinger up in front of my nose as if he were offering me an invisible sweet. I had a terrible headache; I found it hard to keep my eyes open. And what exactly were we so close to, I asked, but Grandfather ignored my question. 'Get dressed,' he said and tossed various items of clothing out of my suitcase onto the bed. 'I'll treat you to breakfast!' But then he only led me down to the hotel buffet. They had nothing but fish on offer—smoked pikes, raw parrotfish, even whole cat sharks gazed at us out of clear eyes from the counter. I only had tea while Grandfather nibbled at a couple of sea urchins and began talking right away.

Yesterday morning in Luoyang, while I was at the post office, he had enlisted the concierge's help to call the Beijing theatre again, where they had promised him three days earlier to keep an ear out for Lian's travelling circus, which Grandfather had told them about. And after many a phone call and many a lead that came to nothing, they had indeed found Dai. Dai had once been an acrobat herself, Grandfather told me, before a severe accident put a premature end to her career. She now worked for a large Shanghai bank, but she had spent the years immediately after her accident in a home for incapacitated artistes—'and that home, now you won't believe this,' said Grandfather, 'was run by Hu.'

Who on earth was Hu, I asked, and Grandfather said he'd tell me that later and went straight on with explaining excitedly how he'd met Dai yesterday, what a delightful person she was, and how he'd told her the whole story about Lian and himself; it had taken all night and in the end Dai had been very touched and had promised to help him.

'What on earth does she want to help you with?' I asked.

And Grandfather said, 'With finding out whether Hu's still alive.' At which he downed another sea urchin and looked out of the window. 'He must be well over a hundred by now,' he added. 'But if anyone can grow old it's him.'

He'd arranged to meet up with Dai again in the evening. 'And until then,' Grandfather announced, 'we're going to have a really great day.'

He had hired us a tandem. 'Everyone in Shanghai rides a bike,' he claimed, although I was convinced of the opposite as soon as we were out on the streets. We were the only people far and wide travelling without a motor, the cars speeding past us frighteningly close. That didn't seem to trouble Grandfather; he pedalled at a leisurely pace (I'd insisted on sitting at the back to make sure he pedalled at all), he whistled some kind of song, which I saw more than heard, and he gazed at the dizzying skyscrapers we pedalled past with a benevolent smile, as though they were flocks of sheep.

Grandfather made the impression he knew where he was steering us. For almost an hour we cycled along identical streets lined with dense rows of high-rises, then we crossed a river and were instantly lost in a tangle of alleyways, crooked houses and tumbledown temples. We had to keep ducking to avoid low-hanging washing lines and there was an acrid stench in the air. 'That's opium,' Grandfather claimed, but I wasn't quite sure whether to believe him. And all of a sudden the thicket of houses grew sparse and we found ourselves at a huge park. 'Here we are then,' said Grandfather, although he sounded rather surprised. We ignored the no bicycles sign—'Ours has two sets of handlebars'—and cycled at walking pace past richly adorned pavilions, perfectly circular ponds, beautifully scented jasmine shrubs, expansive bamboo groves and a huge flowerbed in which various flowers were planted to form a detailed picture of a traditional tea ceremony.

At last we took a break on a bench made out of the protruding roots of a xanhi tree. Before us stretched the jagged contours of Shanghai, a few fauns rollicking on the grass by our side. Grandfather gave a contented sigh. 'Now this is the China I know,' he said.

'You don't know China at all,' I objected, and Grandfather looked offended.

'Just because I've never been here, it doesn't mean I don't know the place,' he said. Lian had told him so much about her home country, in such glowing detail, that it seemed to him as if he'd lived here for years himself. Over all the years, he told me, he'd had dreams about China, often seeing himself bathing in the Yellow River in childhood memories or sitting at the feet of the village elders while they played Chinese folk songs on their unshapely guitars. Sometimes, when something bad had happened, he'd been consoled by the thought that he was in a foreign country, after all, which he'd probably never fully understand. 'This is my home country,' he said, flinging his arm out, 'whether I like it or not.'

How had he understood what Lian told him about China, I asked him. His whole story still seemed fishy to me. Up until then I hadn't had to worry about whether it was true or not, but now that this Hu person had suddenly popped up and turned everything upside down, I was suddenly scared that Grandfather might be getting caught up in something he had possibly made up so long ago that he really did think it was a memory now.

He took two miniature plastic bottles of cognac out of his coat pocket, handed me one and took a cautious sip from the other.

'Communication was indeed difficult to begin with,' he said. From the day when the doctor had made his terrible diagnosis, when Lian had touched Grandfather's cheek, when Grandfather had blushed for the last time in his life, the guards always let him through to the courtyard without further ado. Lian never got up before the afternoon, but Grandfather still waited for her from the early hours every day. 'I've never needed much sleep in my life,' he said, 'but I don't remember ever going to bed during those few weeks.' He paced the courtyard in his agitation, the cigarette butts reaching almost up to his ankles after a few days, and every time Lian was pulled in by her menservants on her wheeled divan, his heart beat so loudly that the window panes began to jingle and jangle.

In the first few days he still barely dared to look at Lian, shyly feeding her with ice cream, pig's knuckles, gateaux, pancakes the size of wagon wheels and entire barrow-loads of potatoes, for which Lian developed a great taste after she overcame her initial scepticism. She now sent her menservants away as soon as she arrived. They would creep into the furthest corner of the courtyard and play quiet games of mah-jong all afternoon, keeping a furtive eye on Grandfather fanning Lian between two bites of food or massaging her shoulders with the paddle. 'We didn't do much talking in the first few days,' said Grandfather. 'But we were still communicating all the time, because everything spoke for itself.' The way she closed her lips round the spoon spoke for itself. The way she turned her neck when he buried the paddle in its folds spoke for itself. The way her eyelashes fluttered when he swung the fan alongside her spoke for itself. It spoke for itself when Grandfather stroked a wisp of hair out of her face now and then, when he tried his best not to sigh out loud when their arms happened to touch, when he breathed in the air when he got close to her hair under some pretext.

'You're a very beautiful woman,' Grandfather sometimes dared to say, and sometimes he said, 'You've got a wonderfully unhealthy appetite,' sometimes even, 'The aftershock from your thighs pursues me into my dreams.' Lian would nod as if she'd understood what he was saying but had to think about it for a while, and then—at times not until half an hour later—she would launch into an answer, purring a few words which, Grandfather hoped, also spoke for themselves, and then there was quiet again. An hour before curtain-up, Lian would be pulled into her changing room, always grasping Grandfather's hand one last time, holding it so tightly that tears came to his eyes, and yet it was even more painful when she let go. For he knew that his knuckles would soon heal but Lian's body would not. Night after night, he sat in the audience and feared that Lian wouldn't appear for her act, but she did appear every time, lifting the weights with ever greater ease, and now her eyes sought Grandfather's immediately during every finale, she threw kisses only in his direction, and Grandfather caught them 'as proudly and greedily as if they were a bride's bouquet'.

A week passed before Lian asked her first question one afternoon. At least, it sounded like a question. She repeated the same sentence several times over, looking at Grandfather invitingly. He tried out several answers. 'Karl,' he said. 'Half past three,' he said. 'In April twenty-three,' he said. 'Cold, but hardly any rain,' he said. But Lian only shook her head every time, asked her question over and over again and finally waved over one of the mah-jong-playing menservants. It was the one who had helped him translate with the doctor, and she whispered something in his ear. The manservant seemed amazed, appeared to require several confirmations that he'd heard correctly and then looked at Grandfather, cleared his throat and said in slow but almost impeccable German, 'Please forgive my directness, but the world sensation Lian wishes me to ask you when, by the belly of Buddha, you are planning to kiss the world sensation Lian finally.' And while Grandfather was still gasping for air, Lian whispered something else to the manservant, which he passed on immediately, 'The world sensation Lian really doesn't wish to appear impatient but, as you doubtlessly know, she does not have long to live and simply has no time for cautious approaches.' Much to his regret, Grandfather was initially speechless.

Finally, he pulled himself together and said to the manservant, 'Would you be so kind as to ask Lian if she'd mind if I kissed her immediately then?'

There was a brief consultation, then the manservant said, 'The world sensation Lian wishes you to know that she wouldn't mind in the slightest.' Perhaps Lian would be so kind as to close her eyes, or else he'd feel rather clumsy, he told the manservant. 'If it helps matters, the world sensation Lian will close her eyes with the greatest of pleasure,' answered the manservant after another brief exchange. Perhaps he, the interpreter, could then also close his eyes, after all it was going to be a rather intimate moment, suggested Grandfather, and he was surprised to hear the manservant translating this too. 'The world sensation Lian has just ordered that all living creatures on land, in water or in the air, single or multi-celled, warm or cold-blooded, laying eggs or giving birth to live offspring, living freely or in captivity, in short, all living creatures on this earth shall immediately close their eyes, in the hope of accelerating the matter somewhat.'

If there had been any room for improvement, Grandfather told me, he'd have fallen even more in love with Lian at that moment than he already was, and he leant over to her but then, noticing he didn't come anywhere close to her mouth through mere leaning, climbed practically on top of her, his hands sinking almost entirely into her cheeks, and pressed his lips to hers. 'She had lips like eiderdowns,' he rhapsodized, 'so warm and soft and fluffy.' And then Lian took his head in both hands—even if he'd wanted to it was now absolutely impossible to end the kiss—and her tongue pushed its way into his mouth and lashed about like a caged reptile, her breasts pressed against his torso with all their might, her right thigh now wrapped so firmly round Grandfather's hips that his legs went numb in a matter of seconds. At some point, she peeled her lips away from his, pressed Grandfather's head to her shoulder and told the manservant to pass on her gratitude and also that she could really do with a bite to eat now. 'And the way she picked the potatoes from my hand with her mouth after that,' said Grandfather, 'not only spoke for itself, it spoke volumes. The kind that get sold in brown paper bags.'

From that day on, not only did they kiss almost unin-terrupted between feeding, massaging and fanning, but the interpreting manservant was always by their side. 'The world sensation Lian wishes you a good morning,' he'd welcome Grandfather as soon as he came rolling into the courtyard with Lian in the early afternoon. 'And if I may be so free,' he added after a few days, 'I personally wish you the same.'

Grandfather took another sip from his cognac bottle. 'And that manservant,' he said once he'd given himself a quick shake, 'was called Hu.'

'The Hu we're looking for?' I asked.

'That very same one.'

It had been a happy week, Grandfather went on, prob-ably the happiest week of his life, although it was a little too soon for that kind of statement. Lian's kisses had been so passionate that he entirely forgot her lips were the lips of a dying woman. Nor did Lian mention her illness with a single word; quite the opposite, the conversations they held with Hu's assistance included more and more plans for the future. Despite both being aware of how impossible they were, they were not going to let that hold them back.

'The world sensation Lian asks whether you could imagine visiting the world sensation Lian one day,' Hu passed on, for instance, and Grandfather answered that it would be a great joy and honour. Because the world sen-sation Lian would like to introduce him to her family, said Hu. That made him very proud and nervous, said Grand-father. 'My own village is very near there, by the way,' said Hu. That was a coincidence, said Grandfather. 'Perhaps you can meet my family too,' said Hu, and Grandfather smiled. 'I'd be delighted.'

Lian and Grandfather got more and more involved in their planning—'The world sensation Lian asks where the honeymoon shall take you'—they thought about setting up their own variety show, they even argued a little over names for children—'The world sensation Lian says she's afraid Gertrud is not at all to her taste'—and only occasionally, when Lian pressed his hand in farewell, did reality shove its way between them again. But it shoved more from day to day, even Hu was usually awkward and silent, only now and then placing a hand on Grandfather's shoulder and whispering in his ear, 'The world sensation Lian now almost certainly says that her grief is as great as the Gobi desert, but her love is fortunately as great as the Gobi desert seen through a magnifying glass.'

On the Sunday of that joyous week there was only a matinee show. The evening was free and unusually mild for the time of year, so Hu suggested they might embark on a little excursion. 'Somewhere where we'll be undisturbed,' he said with a wink in Grandfather's direction. That evening, four menservants pulled Lian to the little cove on the river that Grandfather had chosen, and were then sent to wait in the next cove.

Grandfather had loaded a small snack onto a second cart as a picnic—sandwich loaves, a few cakes, baskets of pears, and after a long search he had even managed to get hold of a barrel of rice wine, which had cost a small fortune.

'I don't want to embarrass you,' Grandfather said to me, handing me his empty cognac bottle and taking my full one in exchange, 'but it did indeed end up being an evening as romantic as it was erotic.' Did I want to know the details, he asked, and I nodded hesitantly, mainly because I got the impression that he rather wanted to tell me about it all.

Hu had lit a small fire by the riverbank, Grandfather told me, and the flames sent excited shadows chasing across Lian's face. She and Grandfather sat tightly intertwined on the divan, eating the delicacies he'd brought along, exchanging childhood memories, kissing and watching in silence as the dark river flowed stubbornly towards the sea.

At some point, Hu took out one of those one-stringed guitars from his homeland and began to play a song, unfamiliar and beautiful, and sang along in a fragile voice. What was the song about, Grandfather wanted to know. 'About a dragon,' explained Hu, 'who loves a fish.' The dragon could not swim, and the fish could not fly, and so they had only ever gazed at each other yearningly through the surface of the sea. Until, one day, their yearning grew so great that the dragon decided to dive into the sea, although it was sure to kill him. At the very same time, however, the fish had decided to jump into the air, although that would surely kill her. And so the dragon dived underwater and drowned at the very moment when the fish suffocated in the air.

'What a sad song,' said Grandfather.

'Not at all,' replied Hu with a few more strokes on his guitar string, while Grandfather took the falling temperature as an excuse to climb deeper and deeper into Lian's pleasantly warm layers. They heard faint laughter from the menservants in the next cove, the river gave off a comforting plashing, now and then the embers of the campfire crackled and Lian's marshmallow hands wandered the length of Grandfather's body. Every spot they had touched begged instantly and desperately for their return. Grandfather kissed Lian's neck and her hilly shoulders and his head migrated between her breasts, which closed over him instantly, robbing him of air but he never wanted to leave that warm, soft, pliable grotto ever again. Lian had undone his trousers and Grandfather pushed aside her robe. He climbed aboard her, her thighs enclosed him, pressing him into her, he was entirely surrounded by flesh, arms, thighs, breasts, the mountain range of her belly pressing close to him, rubbing up against him, flowing round him. Lian sighed, breathed something. 'The world sensation Lian tells you not to stop,' whispered Hu, who was suddenly standing next to them, and Grandfather pressed his hands into the soft mass round him and hooked them into Lian's hair, which was sticking to her body as damp and silky as wet fur.

Lian's breath picked up speed, there was a rattling from her chest, she moaned, 'The world sensation Lian says, "yes",' Hu repeated at shorter and shorter intervals, and then Grandfather heard nothing more, and when he returned to his senses, his arms slung round Lian's neck so as not to be flung from her quaking body, he was suddenly taken captive by such grief that he could not help but cry out loud. 'I know, I know,' said Hu, stroking Grandfather's hair. Lian did not react. She had averted her eyes but Grandfather could see a tear winding its way down her cheek, and he wondered whether it was his own tear from their very first meeting.

All that was left of the fire was the embers. The three of them sat on the divan, Grandfather in the middle, Lian to his right and Hu to his left, all three of them silent. There was no sound from the menservants in the next cove either, they had probably fallen asleep, and even the river roared more quietly, almost coyly.

'I don't want her to die,' Grandfather said to the interpreter.

'Lian says she doesn't want you to die either,' said the interpreter after a brief parley behind Grandfather's back.

'But I'm not going to die,' said Grandfather.

'Lian asks whether you can promise her that.'

Grandfather thought for a while and then nodded. 'I'll see what I can do.'

At that point, he looked at me for the first time during the whole story, gave a brief smile and patted my knee, as if I needed some kind of assurance.

I'd listened to everything with a combination of fascination and puzzlement, yet I must have been so immersed in his story that now as I looked round me again I was suddenly most surprised to find myself here, in China, in Lian's homeland, in Hu's homeland. I felt rather dizzy because Grandfather's confession still seemed like one of his bedtime stories and China was a part of all that, and now I was in the very midst of his invention. I had to think for a long time about what I was imagining and what was real.

'Grandfather?' I asked him.

'Yes?' he answered.

And I said, 'Nothing.' I had just wanted to hear his voice for a moment, to make sure that at least he existed in real life, that he was really sitting here, that he answered 'Yes' and not with a throaty Chinese sound.

'Shall we have something to eat?' he asked, and I nodded and we got back on the tandem. Although we left the park at the same place as we'd come in, we seemed to come out in a completely different part of town. Instead of cycling through crumbling tangles of old alleyways, we now passed along airy tree-lined streets. They were teeming with classy restaurants, fashion boutiques and small bakeries, accordion music came from the open windows of the art deco apartment houses and a group of schoolgirls in uniforms, each holding a globe in one hand, waved and smiled at us.

I was at the back end of the tandem again, trying to give Grandfather directions using the small map in the guidebook. By all appearances, we were in the French concession, Shanghai's most elegant quarter. It wasn't easy to read while cycling—the wind kept flicking the pages over and I kept one hand on the handlebars because of the still dense traffic. Aside from that, Grandfather was constantly pointing out supposed sights—'The opera house on the left,' 'Back there's the oldest brothel in China,' 'Look, a pretty house,'—but as far as I understood the guidebook, Shanghai only grew from a small town to the huge city it undoubtedly is today through maritime trade in the nineteenth century (the name Shanghai means 'built by the sea'). The European influences are correspondingly major;

as well as the French concession there is a Spanish part of town, a Portuguese, an English and a Dutch area. Even the Belgian minority still lives together, although their once expansive quarter has shrunk down over the years to the two middle storeys of an office complex.

I guided us to the harbour area, however, where there are still plenty of nooks and crannies of ill repute but also the true insider's tips among the city's restaurants, according to the guidebook. We settled on the Biyang Zhu (literally, 'he who lies to the wind'), a tiny hut amid huge warehouses. We weren't the only foreigners but we were the only patrons without tattoos. All the exposed body parts were jostling with dragons, anchors and mermaids, and I made out contorted ideographs, bloodied daggers and broken hearts, the occasional sunset, a toothbrush, a woman's name crossed out. No one paid us the slightest attention, which was just fine by us. We took a seat in the only free spot, right at the back by the toilets. I could hardly see Grandfather, so thick was the smoke from the pipes and cigarettes and dried lotus blossoms in the room.

Grandfather rubbed his hand. At last we were away from all the tourist traps, he said, and he gleefully eyed the yellowed posters depicting chastely smiling naked girls, red sports cars, football teams, and one poster with a little kitten curled up in a basket.

Even the waitress was smoking a cigarette as she stared at us, more belligerent than questioning. There didn't seem to be a menu and our English didn't get us very far either, so we simply pointed at the dishes being consumed at an astounding speed at the neighbouring table. The waitress gave a brief nod and turned away, throwing her cigarette to the floor without putting it out, and returned a few minutes later with an unlabelled bottle and two small glasses. She marked the level in the bottle with a pen and then left. Grandfather filled our glasses. 'To Shanghai,' he said.

'To your health,' I said. We drank, and there was an instant burning on my tongue, in my stomach, even in my little toes. I gasped for air, my eyes filling with tears.

'Does you good, eh?' commented Grandfather, topping up the glasses. I shook my head vigorously, saying I ought not to drink any more or I'd guarantee for nothing, but Grandfather pressed the glass into my hand. 'Drink,' he said. 'It's high time you stopped guaranteeing for things.' And yes, goddamn it, he was right, I didn't want to guarantee for anything any more; to be honest I had nothing left to guarantee for. I was in China even though I didn't want to be there, I didn't understand a word, I didn't understand anything else either, I'd lost all grip on our itinerary, I was sitting in a dive somewhere at the end of the world, and all of a sudden I was terribly relieved.

'To me,' I said as I raised my glass.

Grandfather smiled. 'To you,' he said.

I've forgotten how many more glasses we emptied before our food finally arrived, two bowls filled well beyond the brim, from which protruded all manner of pincers and tentacles and eyes and fins, none of which we could identify. That didn't bother us though; we gobbled it all up between enthusiastic toasts to the chef, to Shanghai, to China with all its delicious flora and fauna. The gap between the top of the liquid and the pen marking grew larger and larger, partly because we didn't always hit the glasses when we poured, and at some point Grandfather shook the last few drops out of the bottle. 'To the world sensation Lian,' I said.

Grandfather gave a grateful nod. 'To Lian,' he said, and then he started to cry, at first quietly, barely audibly, and then it all came gushing out and he sobbed at the top of his lungs, his whole body quaking, fluid running out of his eyes, his nose, his mouth, and I sat opposite him helpless and drunk, occasionally stroking his arm and wishing I could join the crying.

After a while one of the generously tattooed men from the next table wordlessly handed him a handkerchief. It was obviously used; nevertheless, Grandfather blew his nose on it at great length, wiped his face on it and then looked at me out of tiny eyes. 'I think I need a bit of a lie down,' he said. Then his head slumped onto the table and I pushed the glasses swiftly aside before I lay mine down too.

Upon waking I expected the headache I deserved but I felt none. In fact I felt surprisingly refreshed. Grandfather seemed to be in fine form as well. He was sitting at one of the other tables, playing cards with a handful of sailors and just gathering up a pile of banknotes when he caught sight of me. 'Good thing you're awake,' he called over. 'We've got to get going.' He shook hands with every one of his card-playing chums, one of whom even called something after him, and all the others laughed. Grandfather joined in. 'Nice lads,' he said once we got outside. 'No good at cards, but really nice lads.'

We had to get a move on now though, said Grandfather. He had arranged to pick Dai up from work. However, the effect of all the liquor came back to us on the tandem and we careened recklessly through the traffic, regularly falling over when we leant in opposite directions at junctions, Grandfather sometimes stopping pedalling altogether and gradually tipping to one side, then I trying to right him with one hand. 'Everything's under control,' he'd call out quickly.

Although Grandfather claimed to know the way exactly, by the time we passed the three-legged Oriental Pearl Tower for the fourth time I no longer believed his claim that Shanghai was absolutely full of these towers. We stopped a taxi, and after multiple exchanges of words and banknotes Grandfather convinced the driver to strap our tandem to the roof.

Grandfather got very agitated again in the taxi. 'You'll like Dai,' he said.

'If you say so,' I said.

'She can light a cigarette with a match between her toes,' he said.

'That must come in handy,' I said.

'And hold the cigarette between her toes when she smokes.'

'Aha,' I said.

'With her legs crossed behind her head,' he said. Had she showed him, I asked, and Grandfather shook his head. 'No, but I'm certain she can do it all.'

In the end, we arrived at the bank where Dai worked, more than three-quarters of an hour late for our appointment. The street looked abandoned apart from a single young woman sitting on the pavement in the lotus position. 'That's her,' Grandfather exclaimed and ran straight up to her as I was still unfastening the tandem from the taxi roof.

'Dai, this is Keith. Keith, this is Dai,' he said, beaming at us in expectation. Not using her arms, Dai leapt to her feet and held a hand out to me. 'Keith,' she said, 'what a nice name.'

She was older than I'd thought at first glance, in her early or perhaps even mid-thirties. Her body was wiry, almost boyish, her hair cropped short and both her upper canines made of gold, sending brief glints of light from her mouth with every word.

She gave Grandfather a kiss on the cheek. 'Did you find anything out?' he asked. Dai smiled. She'd tell him all about it in a moment but first she wanted to get a bite to eat, she said. Were we as hungry as she was, she asked, and I nodded even though the thought of food made me dizzy.

We got on our tandem, Dai perched on the rear handlebars, and off we set. How did I like Shanghai, she asked me, and I said it was a very multifaceted city. 'Yes,' said Dai and nodded sadly; she was afraid I was right. She knew her way round amazingly well. Between the instructions she called out to Grandfather—'Now turn left,' 'Turn right after two hundred metres,' 'Follow the road,'—she kept pointing out the sights we cycled past, and almost every building in Shanghai seemed to be a sight. She showed us the Temple of Confucius, the Jade Buddha Temple and the Temple of Five Lords, she showed us the Ohel Moishe Synagogue, the Customs House and the Peace Hotel, she showed us the City Museum, the City Planning Museum, the Museum Planning Museum, she showed us the allegedly most expensive hairdressing salon in China, she showed us the allegedly smallest skyscraper in Asia, she showed us the cutest dog in the world.

And so as to show us all of this all the better, at some point along the way she stood up on the handlebars. I noticed that one of her legs seemed to be shorter than the other. She was wearing a flat shoe on her left foot, and on her right one a high heel, with a difference of a good two inches.

'Here it is,' said Dai all of a sudden, leaping off the handlebars, and we followed her into a building that looked like an amusement arcade from the outside, and from the inside, as we soon found out, also like an amusement arcade. There were long cramped rows of flashing fruit machines, a middle-aged Chinese man perched on a bar stool in front of each. Dai strode across the room, opened a plain, unlabelled door at the opposite end, and we walked into a kitchen. Frying pans were tossed about on a large stove, alongside it two sweaty men chopping vegetables on a trestle table. A huge aquarium occupied almost the entire back wall, with hundreds of fish, crustaceans and cephalopods jostling for space in its greenish water. In the middle of the kitchen were five plastic tables, all occupied, but Dai called something out and a waitress instantly brought another table, resolutely shoved the others aside and asked us to take a seat. It was incredibly hot in the kitchen. There was a large ceiling fan but it rotated too slowly to make any difference; we were sitting so close together that I was constantly being jabbed in the back by the chopsticks in use at the next table; the woks hissed, the cooks yelled, and there was a radio turned up loud somewhere. 'So,' said Dai, 'now we can talk about everything in peace at last.'

At first, however, all we talked about was food. I did mention that all I wanted was a salad at the most, but Dai only snorted in contempt, then took Grandfather and me by the hand and led us to the fish tank. 'What takes your fancy?' she asked and as we stared cluelessly at the aquatic hustle and bustle she called the waitress over and began to order for all three of us. Over and over, she had the waitress fish out a crab, an octopus or a jellyfish to inspect them close up. By the end she had chosen over a dozen of them. 'You two want beer, don't you?' she asked on the way back to the table and waved three raised fingers at the waitress, not waiting for our answer.

'So what did you find out?' asked Grandfather once the beer bottles were on the table. Dai took a long swig, wiped her mouth and smiled proudly. She had made a lot of calls today, she said. It hadn't been easy but after countless conversations with acquaintances of acquaintances of acquaintances she'd finally found someone who could help her. Hu was very old by now but he was still running the home and after numerous relocations in recent years it was currently in Fenghuang, apparently, which was a fortunate coincidence because that was only eight hundred kilometres away.

Grandfather, excited, tore strips off the label on his beer bottle. What was the quickest way to get there, he asked. Dai thought for a moment. 'I suggest we hire a car,' and Grandfather abandoned his bottle.

'We?' he asked. Dai looked from him to me and back again. She'd come with us, of course, she said. Or did we mind?

'Not in the slightest,' I said.

'Au contraire,' said Grandfather.

Dai raised her bottle to ours. 'Great, then we'll just have a bite to eat first.'

Grandfather and I were speechless and Dai seemed to like that. 'You've seen almost all of Shanghai now. If we leave right away we'll be there by lunchtime tomorrow.'

Then our food came. Dai loaded up her bowl and began to eat calmly, I just nibbled a little at a beansprout and Grandfather didn't touch any of it. But I could see he was smiling.

It's very easy to hire a car in China. We pushed the tandem to the next junction and when the lights turned red Dai pointed at the waiting cars. 'Choose one,' she said and then—although Grandfather had decided on a sports car with blue-tinted windows—she walked up to a more than dented pickup, knocked at the window and began talking at the driver. After a few minutes of heated negotiations she handed the driver a pile of money, whereupon he got out of the car, gave Grandfather and me a sceptical look, then checked the tandem's tyre pressure, climbed on and cycled off without a word. 'That's that then,' said Dai, sitting down behind the wheel. Grandfather got the seat next to her and I squeezed onto the cramped back seat. I told Dai we had to pick up our luggage from the hotel, but she said we had no time for that.

'We'll get it on the way back.'

We've been driving for almost three hours now, at least half of which we spent getting out of Shanghai. Now we're passing through a huge industrial area with endless rows of tall chimneys on either side. Dai has switched on the fog lights but we still can't see far at all. She and Grandfather are whispering rather a lot. I can't understand what they're saying. Sometimes they laugh, sometimes Dai strokes his head for a while.

I'm going to try and get some sleep now.

I wonder how you all are.

See you very soon,

K.

I wasn't used to sitting on the train, wasn't used to moving, wasn't used to being surrounded by so many people suddenly, people who could see me, although they seldom made use of the opportunity. I still nodded at every one of them though.

I had to change trains after forty-five minutes, and all at once I hoped the second train wouldn't be a regional train, hoped a stream engine would come puffing along instead, gone astray from the Trans-Siberian Railway. I hoped I'd be sitting alone in a compartment, before me a steaming samovar, and countryside would pass by the window for days, forests and fields and mountains and deserts, and I wouldn't disembark until China—with quite some delay but better than never.

But, of course, all that arrived was the regional express. I got on the train, and all that passed by the windows was the Westerwald, and I was familiar enough with that from my grandfather's postcards. And he couldn't have wanted to stay there, that couldn't have been his plan. And he must have had a plan that had then been unexpectedly foiled. He must have had a destination that was then never reached. Because the only thing that made me sadder than the fact that he hadn't completed his intentions, whatever they may have been, was the possibility that perhaps he had completed them, that possibly nothing had been easier than completing everything because there hadn't been any real plan at all, because in the end he simply hadn't cared, just like at some point he hadn't cared about so much, almost everything in fact. But seeing as he'd set out so dramatically on this one last journey, as if he wasn't a hamster at all but an elephant, seeing as he'd tried to cover his tracks, seeing as he'd absolutely insisted on being lost without a trace, he could at least have got himself a little further away, because the Westerwald was a very tricky place to get lost without a trace.

The pathology department was in the basement—where else? The corridor was deathly quiet, my shoes squeaking far too loudly on the linoleum. I didn't want to be heard, I didn't want to be seen, I didn't want the corridor to come to an end. I wanted it to go on for ever, extending once round the whole world, the arrows on the signs only indicating a direction and no destination. But, of course, the frosted glass door came along at some point, with 'Please ring the bell once only' on a sign next to it, which seemed rather unnecessary—who was in a rush round here? I took a few calming deep breaths, even ran my hand through my hair as if embarking on some kind of official visit and readied myself for the worst.

I'd never seen a dead person. My only experience of death had been Friedrich or Vincent, our short-term cat. Only my grandfather was with him when the vet gave him his injection. We grandchildren had to stay in the waiting room, which was fine by us. I remember us assuming sad expressions when my grandfather joined us with the lifeless Friedrich or Vincent cradled in his arm, but mainly because we knew that was the thing to do. My grandfather, though, was absolutely distraught. 'I actually heard the life leaving his body,' he told us on the way home. It had been a quiet sound, a sort of clicking—and he looked round the car for comparisons, opened and closed the glove compartment a few times and said, 'Like that, but even quieter.'

Once we got home he told us to clear the dining table so that we could lay out Friedrich or Vincent on it. We grandchildren wanted to bury him as soon as possible but my grandfather insisted on us all viewing the corpse, for at least an hour—we owed it to the cat, he said. 'Take a very good look at him,' said my grandfather. 'He'll never be alive again. He'll never chase another bird again, he'll never stretch again, he'll never purr again, he'll never lick his paws, he'll never close his eyes, he'll never smell anything, he'll never taste anything, he'll never plan anything, he'll never be happy again, he'll never be sad again, he'll never want anything again, he'll never be in pain again, he'll never hope anything, he'll never feel that emptiness inside, he'll never get a day older, he'll never regret anything, he'll never miss anything, he'll be certain at last that from now on nothing can get any worse.' One by one, we all started crying and my grandfather stopped talking, gazing at Friedrich or Vincent with a look I couldn't quite categorize. There was a great deal of tiredness in it, at any rate.

We were allowed to bury the cat at last once the hour was up. Each of us said a few words, only my grandfather refusing when it came to his turn. 'He can't hear us,' he said. 'He never could, he was a cat.' And then he went back inside the house and we saw no sign of him for the rest of the day.

I pressed the bell. I pressed it a second time and a third time, not even stopping when I heard hurried footsteps from inside, when I heard 'All right, all right', still ringing when the door was jerked open and the pathologist gave me an evil glare. She didn't look at all as I'd imagined her on the telephone. She was thirty at the most, tanned, with a small rhinestone glinting from the left wing of her nose. Couldn't I read, she asked, and although I told her that yes, I could read, she had to forcibly remove my finger from the bell in the end. 'What's the matter?' she asked after that.

'I'm Keith Stapperpfennig. We spoke on the phone.'

The pathologist raised her eyebrows. 'Glad you could make it,' she said, obviously trying her best to sound genuine. Then she turned on her heel and walked along the narrow corridor, opened a double door and let me go through first.

The room was smaller than I'd expected but otherwise everything looked the way I thought it would. There was the neon light, there was the bareness, there was the coldness and the humming sound. The refrigerator covered almost the entire left wall, complete with about twenty metal drawers. I wondered how many of them were occupied.

The suntanned pathologist headed straight for one of the drawers on the bottom right and tugged it open with both hands. I held my breath, thinking my grandfather was about to glide towards me naked and shrunken, but I'd forgotten the white body bag that I ought to have known about from films. Something that must have been feet made a bump at the far end but other than that the bag had no contours, thank goodness. The pathologist looked at me. 'Are you ready?' she asked, and she probably had to ask that but there really was something like empathy in her voice. I nodded, although it wasn't true. Of course I wasn't ready, when was anyone ever ready, and of course it was an absolutely ridiculous question. She'd have been better off saying 'Watch out,' or 'Good luck.' And then she pulled the zip down a little way and I saw my grandfather's hair, my grandfather's forehead, I saw his bushy eyebrows, his closed eyelids, I saw his broad nose, his narrow lips, I saw his square chin, I saw his wrinkled neck, and there my gaze ended; the bag was only unzipped as far as that. I felt the pathologist's eyes on me. I mustn't close my eyes, I mustn't sigh or scream or sob, I mustn't look for too long, I thought, but what I really wanted was to look for terribly long, for at least an hour, I wanted to not miss a thing, to imprint it all on my mind, every spot on his skin, every wrinkle, every single hair. He looked younger than over the past few months, rather pale of course, with two deep lines formed between his nose and the corners of his mouth, but otherwise he seemed recuperated, almost as if he was enjoying himself, as if his head wasn't protruding from a body bag but from a bubble bath.

The pathologist cleared her throat. I looked up at her and smiled.

'That's not my grandfather.'

23 May, Fenghuang

My dears,

What a lovely day today was, the best on our whole
trip, the best of all for a long time. I'm lying in bed on my
own in a hostel room in Fenghuang, trying to ignore the
noises from the room next door. Our trip will no doubt be
over tomorrow, no matter what happens. And all at once
that makes me feel sad. I'll miss China, I'll miss Grandfather in China, I'll even miss Dai, even though I've only
known her for such a short time.

Like me, you've probably been wondering for a while
how Dai speaks such good German. I asked her about it in
the car last night, and she gave me a surprised look. 'Oh,
that's German?' As it turned out, Dai speaks at least a
dozen languages. She'd travelled a lot as a young girl and
Shanghai is a pretty international city, she told us. But
when it came to most of the languages she spoke, she
didn't know what they were called or where they were
used. Then she asked lots of eager questions and Grandfather and I told her a lot about Germany, about the landscape, the history, the politics, the music, the food, and Dai
listened wide-eyed and then laughed and said, 'Come now,
you're making all that up as you go along.'

Dai woke me after a few hours' sleep. Would I take over
the driving, she asked; it was only straight ahead for the

next five or six hours. We swapped places and Dai fell asleep on the spot. Grandfather's eyes were closing too but I didn't want to sit there alone, I didn't want to be his chauffeur as usual. So I said to him, 'You still owe me the end of your story.' Grandfather blinked. He'd tell me tomorrow, he said, but I was having none of it. 'I'm driving hundreds of miles to a place not even remotely on our itinerary, in the middle of the night,' I said, and I pointed out that I had a right to find out what exactly he was looking for. And apart from that, he seemed to have told Dai everything already, which was not fair at all.

Grandfather rubbed his eyes, sat up straight, nodded a few times and then said, 'If I knew exactly what I was looking for I'd have told you long ago.' He took a sleepy look out of the window. The industrial buildings were behind us and now we were driving through almost empty countryside. Towns we didn't know the names of gave off a faint light in the distance. There was hardly any traffic, only the occasional truck overtaking us, a cattle transport, a loudly ringing bicycle.

'Lian is dead,' said Grandfather after a long while. 'And it's all so long ago that I sometimes fear I've made the whole thing up.' He looked at me. 'All I want is a memory I can reach out and touch, do you see?' His time with Lian had been terribly short but, of course, they hadn't wanted to admit that to each other, and so he had no keepsakes from that time, no love letters, no locks of hair, no dried potato peels, no pebbles from their evening together by the river.

That night of love, said Grandfather, remained their only one, for both of them knew that a night as carefree as that could never be repeated. Grandfather had descended into a debilitating sadness. He could hardly look at Lian the next afternoon; suddenly the signs of her sickness could no longer be ignored. She grew paler from day to day, deep bags forming under her eyes, her hair falling out by the tuft, her fingernails breaking, and from then on she gave off a permanent sickly sweet scent. To this day, Grandfather said, he couldn't stand condensed milk.

Lian was still going on stage every night but her weights were getting lighter and lighter, the finale with the pyramid was even struck out of the show entirely, and now and then all she did was lift the first few dumb-bells and then exit without as much as a bow. The audiences grew restless and then began to grumble, despite the acrobats immediately tumbling back onto the stage, improvising formations to distract them from the failed finale.

In the afternoons too, Grandfather told me, Lian was now enveloped in an oppressive melancholia, expressed above all in her eating behaviour. It was only with great persuasion that Grandfather managed to force a few spoonfuls of ice cream upon Lian, half a cake, perhaps a handful of potatoes. Her chins reduced rapidly in number and her silken robe puckered and wrinkled, while Lian spoke very little, so little that Hu kept feeling the need to interrupt her silences with explanations such as 'The world sensation Lian still has nothing to say.'

And at some point, Grandfather could no longer cope. 'Come, let's go away, somewhere you've always wanted to go,' he suggested, but Lian did nothing more than shrug. She'd been everywhere already, she said. 'Then we'll buy you whatever you've always wished for,' but once again Lian's reaction was cool. There was nothing she wanted any more, she said. Grandfather made plenty more suggestions but Lian had already eaten everything she'd ever wanted to eat, she'd smelt everything she'd ever wanted to smell, discussed everything there was to discuss, she had said everything, heard everything, played everything, claimed everything, corrected everything, felt everything already. 'Is there really nothing at all,' asked Grandfather, 'not even one single unfulfilled wish?' For a long time, Lian eyed the potatoes in her hand, and then she smiled and whispered something. Grandfather saw Hu biting his cheek to stop himself from laughing out loud.

'Lian is just remembering,' Hu said with as much self-control as possible, 'how she always dreamt as a child of becoming a tightrope walker.'

Grandfather didn't know what was so funny about that. He gave an earnest nod. 'And walk the tightrope you shall,' he said, not even waiting for Hu to translate. 'You'll be walking the tightrope by the end of the week. It'll be the greatest finale ever to be seen at a variety theatre, the audience will cheer so loudly for you that we'll have to hand out earplugs, they'll still be applauding even days, no, weeks later.' Grandfather couldn't stop making promises, he was so glad to have finally found an objective, a way out, instead of simply waiting and watching the Massif of Macau crumbling away before his very eyes.

Hu could hardly keep up with his translations. He too was getting louder and louder, more and more excessive, making Grandfather suspect he was adding even more embellishments to what he'd said himself. Lian listened to it all impassively and then simply shook her head slowly. But Grandfather refused to accept that shake of her head, obviously oblivious to that kind of thing even back then. 'We'll start tomorrow,' he said and leapt to his feet to get started on the preparations right away. 'Make sure you get a good night's sleep, it's going to be a tough day,' he called to Lian, and then he left the courtyard and the theatre, not noticing he was whistling until a few blocks further on.

Grandfather had started yawning again and slumped down on the passenger seat, his eyes now closed. 'Don't you dare fall asleep,' I said. I turned the ventilation up as high as it would go.

'Even if I do,' said Grandfather, 'I know the story so well I can tell it in my sleep.' And, in fact, he did jerk several times as he carried on talking, letting off the occasional snore, but he spoke with no significant pauses. Quite the opposite, the words flowed into one another and only sometimes did he swallow a few final syllables.

The next day he had returned to the courtyard early on, he told me as I stared in concentration at the arrow-straight road ahead. To tell the truth, he said, there hadn't been much to prepare. They had to start slowly and carefully, and his first step would be merely to introduce Lian to the rope. He lay it out on the ground diagonally from one corner of the courtyard to the other, and when Lian was brought in on her divan early that afternoon, he served her only a few spoonfuls of ice cream and then asked her to try a few steps along the low rope. 'Nothing can happen,' he said. Lian looked at the rope for a while, then her head slumped to her chest again. There was no point, she communicated to Grandfather, and he leapt to his feet again. Of course there was a point, nothing else had a point, there had never been so much point, and he walked along the rope and back again with his arms outstretched, only losing his footing once or twice. 'Look,' he exclaimed, 'it's quite simple.'

But Lian hadn't even been watching, and when Grandfather sat back down next to her Hu gave him a consolatory pat on the back. 'There's not enough time,' said Hu. 'It's too late.'

But Grandfather didn't want it to be too late. He shook his head mutely for almost an hour, then, all at once, he nodded. 'You're both right,' he said. 'There's not enough time. We can't afford to start so slowly and carefully.' And he got up again, picked up the rope, ran up to the third floor of the theatre and stretched it from one window of the stairwell right across the courtyard to another window. 'Come on,' he called down to Lian, 'it's child's play.' After a brief translation Hu called back that Lian wasn't a child any more, and Grandfather called, 'All the better!' because then she needn't be nearly as scared, and the rope was strong enough, he promised, and Hu called that Lian said Grandfather could go first, and Grandfather called back, 'All right,' and before he could think better of it he'd climbed out of the window and found himself, both arms flailing, on the tautly stretched rope.

By this point, Grandfather had opened his eyes again and was looking at me from the passenger seat. 'I'd never been so frightened in my life,' he said. His pulse, his knees, his guts, his hands, all made it more than clear that he didn't belong up there. He swayed so strongly that the left and right walls of the courtyard came racing towards him by turn. 'And then,' he said, 'I saw Lian.' Even from thirty feet up, her body was huge. Her head tipped way back, she was gazing up at him, her mouth so wide open that he could see deep down her oesophagus, and all signs of melancholy had disappeared from her eyes. All they reflected was sheer terror. 'And all at once I knew I mustn't fall,' said Grandfather. And his pulse, his knees, his guts and his hands knew it too and instantly stopped thudding, stopped trembling, stopped wrenching and sweating. 'I have no memory of the next few seconds of my life,' said Grandfather. He only came to once he'd reached the opposite window, once he'd climbed into the stairwell and collapsed in a trembling heap. 'I must have lain there for half an hour,' said Grandfather, and then he'd got to his feet, combed his hair, taken a few deep breaths and returned to the courtyard, whistling a tune. 'Every thing's shipshape up there,' he told a still stunned Lian, and then he told her it was her turn now, and Lian turned round to Hu and had a long talk with him, and then the two of them nodded, only once each and not very emphatically, but that was enough for Grandfather. With Hu's assistance, he instantly began building a ramp and while all the available menservants pulled the divan up the stairs he ran to the opposite window to await Lian at the other end of the rope.

He waited a long time, and just as he was about to go down again she stepped out onto the windowsill. She filled it entirely, and although she was about fifteen metres away from Grandfather he could see just how her eyes were flickering, how her nostrils were flaring, how her lower arms were coming out in goosepimples. 'Look at me, don't look at anything else,' he called out, and Lian did just that, did nothing else and moved not one inch. 'Just start walking,' said Grandfather, 'as if you'd forgotten something over here with me and you just have to come back for it quickly.' He heard Hu's voice faintly but Lian still didn't budge. Grandfather called out all sorts of other things, called until he was hoarse, but Lian stayed put all along, her eyes affixed on Grandfather. Then it was time to get ready for the evening's performance. Lian left the window frame and Grandfather received her down in the courtyard. 'Maybe tomorrow,' Hu translated, and Lian stroked Grandfather's cheek gently as if it was he who needed consoling.

The next day, Lian did not set foot on the rope either. She had the menservants lug her up to the window as soon as she arrived, but this time too she spent all afternoon frozen to the spot, although Grandfather called out even louder, although he held up encouraging placards, although he pleaded and threatened and spurred and swore and enticed her with any number of delicacies. Lian wouldn't move as much as a finger, and down in the court-yard she had Hu tell him 'Maybe tomorrow,' again, and Grandfather said, 'Yes, maybe tomorrow,' and folded up his encouraging placards.

'That day was the only time I missed one of Lian's per-formances,' said Grandfather. Though he'd known he'd regret it bitterly afterwards, he simply hadn't been able to watch. He lay on his bed and stared at the ceiling, hearing the muffled sound of the final applause from downstairs, and a little later there was a knock at the door. Grandfather didn't say 'Come in,' but Hu came in shyly nonetheless.

'Where were you?' he asked. Lian had been very dis-appointed not to see him. Grandfather said he was very disappointed himself. 'By what?' asked Hu, sitting down on the edge of the bed. Grandfather folded his arms. 'By the fact that Lian's not even trying to fulfil her last wish.' Hu sat very straight, the palms of his hands resting precisely parallel to one another on his thighs. He cleared his throat. 'I'm not entirely sure whether it's Lian's last wish or yours.' Then he stood up, bowed and left the room, and Grandfather was left behind alone, and he'd never felt as small as he did at that moment—'as small as the dot on an *i* in a name written on a grain of rice.'

He vowed not to even mention tightrope walking the next day, so he was all the more surprised when he walked into the courtyard and saw Lian already poised on the windowsill. He hurried to take up his position at the other end of the rope, not calling anything out, not holding anything up, not enticing her with anything, and two hours later Lian, her eyes fixed on Grandfather, cautiously lifted her left foot from the sill and placed it on the rope. There it stayed, inching forward bit by bit, sometimes on its toes, sometimes on its heel, its huge toes snaking round the thin rope, and Grandfather tried to smile but either he failed or Lian didn't even notice it. Certainly she didn't smile back. At some point her left foot had inched so far along the rope that she had to stretch her leg right out, standing in a lunge, her arms already straight out on either side, her head already in the open air, but her right foot simply refusing to lose contact with the windowsill, and dusk fell, and the make-up artists complained, and bit by bit Lian inched her left foot back and disappeared out of the window frame, and down in the courtyard she didn't say 'Maybe tomorrow,' because the next day was the last performance. They were facing their farewell, 'And there was no doubt,' said Grandfather, 'that it would be a final farewell.' He said that very quietly, and he said, 'The next day, our last day, I looked for . . .' even more quietly, and then he said nothing at all. He'd fallen asleep. No matter how hard I shook him he wouldn't wake up, his snores loud and even, the morning breaking outside. I wanted to drive straight on and on, straight on for ever, across the Gobi Desert, across the Himalayas, along the Silk Road, I wanted to have no destination. Now and then Dai or Grandfather might wake up and ask, 'Are we nearly there yet?' and I'd say, 'Not quite yet.'

The landscape filled up again, the houses got larger, the traffic got busier, and then I saw Dai waking up in the rear-view mirror. She blinked a few times and looked out of the window. 'I can take over again now,' she said.

Early in the afternoon we reached Fenghuang's city wall. It still forms a closed circle round the town, although it's fallen into such ruin at some points that it barely reaches knee height. 'Let's get a bite to eat,' Dai suggested. We parked the car and joined forces to wake Grandfather.

'Where am I?' he asked, looking round in confusion.

'Almost at the destination,' said Dai, and Grandfather seemed to remember now, and smiled, but only for a moment, and then looked at the ground in fear.

'At the destination,' he repeated.

We found a small cafe, where the walls were plastered from floor to ceiling with autograph cards, and ate a late breakfast—dumplings filled with a sweet ginger paste with the surprising accompaniment of rose hip tea. Dai ate nothing, only smoked a cigarette. I was disappointed to see her using her hands to do so. Grandfather looked at the people on the autograph cards. 'They all look the same to me,' he said, and Dai said that was no wonder, they were all of the same person.

Who was it, I asked, and Dai shrugged. 'No idea,' she said. Then she looked at her watch, put out her cigarette and said we ought to start looking for the artistes' home. I nodded; only Grandfather seemed to be in no rush whatsoever, all of a sudden. Couldn't he eat his breakfast in peace, he asked, chewing his last mouthful at a speed uncharacteristically slow for him.

The old heart of Fenghuang is divided right down the middle by the Tuojiang River. On either side, the houses are built on stilts along the banks, some of them so high you can only reach the front doors by rope ladder. The narrow streets were crowded with groups of Chinese tourists, with souvenir stalls every few yards selling mostly small plastic phoenixes, and we also saw all kinds of street artists, musicians, jugglers, conjurers, fortune tellers, sword swallowers and artistes. Dai spoke to every one of them, returning to us after less than an hour with a huge smile on her face. 'I've found it,' she said. It was a little way outside of town but if we hurried we could make it that same day.

'Wonderful,' I said, and Grandfather said the same, just that he urgently had to buy a couple of phoenixes first.

I caught up with him at a souvenir stall. What was the matter with him, I asked, and he spent some time inspecting one of the red plastic birds. 'Perhaps I'm not quite ready yet,' he said.

'Ready for what?' I asked.

Grandfather stroked the phoenix's long beak gingerly. 'For our journey to be over already,' he said. I took the bird out of his hand and put it back down on the table. That was what he'd come for though, I said. Grandfather nodded. Yes, he said, but he hadn't known that beforehand.

In the meantime, Dai had rented a new car for us, this time a small Japanese model. She hooted and held the passenger door open. 'Are we ready?' she asked.

I looked at Grandfather, and he gazed at the ground, tense with the strain. 'Perhaps we ought to wait until tomorrow after all,' I said.

Dai hesitated for a moment and then turned off the engine. 'You're right,' she said. 'We've got plenty of time.'

We strolled round the streets of Fenghuang a little longer, and although we only took casual notice of the almost entirely ruined temples and pagodas, city towers and bridges, it was still very much the best day of our trip so far, whereby the competition admittedly wasn't so great. Grandfather seemed much more relaxed now. We walked along the riverbank, one of us on either side of Dai, who linked arms with us. The evening sun shone on our faces, the fishermen waved from the river and we waved back.

A band was playing in a small park and Grandfather asked Dai for a dance. They made a wonderful sight; the songs grew faster and faster and the two of them whirled round more and more breathlessly, Dai's false teeth flashing more and more often until they seemed to form a golden ring round them.

They joined me again fully out of breath. 'You must be glad to have a Grandfather like him,' said Dai as we were leaving the park.

'Yes,' I said, not knowing whether I really was glad or not. But I wanted to be; there was nothing I wanted more than that. Everyone else managed it so it couldn't be all that difficult, surely.

We took two rooms in the Hongqiao Bian Kezhan, a good-value hostel with a view of the river. We ate our evening meal there too, Dai ordering for us again. 'You do like racoon?' she asked, not waiting for an answer. In fact, I've long since lost all my inhibitions when it comes to food, and Grandfather didn't complain either. 'Racoon,' he repeated, as if it was a Chinese word he'd just learnt.

Didn't he want to finish telling me the story about Lian, I asked him while Dai was busy sending an astounding number of text messages. Grandfather gave me a surprised look. He'd finished the story in the car, he said. 'No,' I said, 'you fell asleep.'

'Really?' asked Grandfather. He must have dreamt the rest of it then.

Dai looked up from her phone without interrupting her typing. 'You haven't finished telling him the story yet?' she asked, appalled. Grandfather shook his head; something had always got in the way. 'For more than twenty years?'

'Yes,' said Grandfather, 'I'm afraid so.' But now he was going to finally finish what he'd started. Where had he got to, he asked me.

'Your last day together,' I said, and Grandfather nodded a few times.

'The last day,' he said. 'How strange that it didn't all happen yesterday.'

He hadn't slept the night before, of course, and he'd spent all morning pacing restlessly round town trying to distract himself, but it hadn't worked. The hours up to the early afternoon passed unbearably slowly, yet at the same time not slowly enough; it was to be the last time he'd ever wait for Lian.

When he returned to the Tamtam he found everyone in a state of great agitation. At first he thought it must just be because of the approaching departure, but then he was told why everyone was in such a flurry—Lian had disappeared, cleared out her room, and there was no trace of Hu either. The circus director was throwing a tantrum in his caravan. Grandfather heard him sobbing, heard him shouting, heard crockery smashing, and he almost felt like asking if he needed a hand.

A waiter brought our racoons and Dai put her phone down, but none of us started eating. Grandfather picked up his chopsticks and started rubbing them against each other as he went on with his story.

'I looked for Lian everywhere,' he said, 'in every room in the building.' He had called all the hospitals, to no avail, thankfully, and then he'd gone round to all the potato sellers, all the ice cream parlours and bakeries and butcher's shops, but no one had seen her. He had even gone out to the river again, to the spot where they'd had their picnic, and he'd been 'most offended' not to find her there either.

It would have made the perfect place for their farewells, and now it looked as if there wouldn't be any farewells at all. Perhaps it was best that way; after all, they had done nothing but say their farewells for the whole two weeks; they had only got to know each other in the first place because of a farewell, and from the next day on they'd be half a world apart and soon enough even further than that.

That evening's performance did not go well. Everyone on stage seemed distracted, making unwarranted mistakes, and the closer the finale came, the less they could conceal their anxiety, which quickly infected the audience. A murmuring spread round the auditorium, soon swelling to a rustling, a whispering, a barely subdued speaking, and by the time the director finally came on stage to announce that the world sensation Lian had sadly been taken ill Grandfather could barely understand him, what with all the talking and whistling and coughing and complaining round him.

The acrobats tumbled listlessly back on stage to give the show at least some sense of an ending but no one paid them any attention. Grandfather got up and headed for the exit. All he wanted was to go to bed, but just as he reached the door the noise died down so suddenly that he thought he must have gone deaf from one moment to the next. He turned round and saw the entire audience looking to the front, spellbound. It couldn't be because of the acrobats—their pyramid had long since collapsed and they were lying scattered across the stage, staring upwards. And then Grandfather spotted Lian. Thirty feet above the stage, she was standing on the tiny platform at the end of the tightrope. She was wearing a plain white robe and, as far as Grandfather could make out, no make-up. Next to her, pushed terrifyingly close to the edge, was Hu, gripping Lian's left hand. In the other hand she held a ridiculously small sunshade.

For a moment Grandfather was rooted to the spot. 'Fear and joy blocked each other's view by turns within me,' he told me. Then he ran along the aisle, leapt onto the stage and climbed up the thin ladder to the platform at the other end of the rope as quickly as he could. The wooden structure beneath his feet swayed ominously. It must have been much worse on Lian's side. He looked over at her, seeking her gaze and was shocked when he didn't find it. Her eyes were open and she was looking at him, yet he could make out nothing in them, no fear, no joy, no sorrow, no love, no triumph, no exhaustion, 'not even indifference', said Grandfather, rubbing his chopsticks together so hard that I feared I'd soon see sparks and smoke. 'It was as if the well I had always looked into had suddenly been bricked up.'

The artistes on and behind the stage had overcome their initial horror and were now running to and fro in their agitation, all calling Lian's name and a confusion of other things Grandfather didn't understand. Now they began to climb up the ladder to Lian's platform. For a while Hu managed to fend them off with his feet but then the first of them caught hold of Lian's robe, others were soon grabbing for her bones, the sword swallower tried to cut the high wire with a long blade, the trapeze artistes formed a human lasso in mid-air, and then Lian set off.

Apart from Grandfather, everyone in the theatre was just waiting for the wire to break instantly beneath Lian's weight. Most of them will never know why it didn't. 'But they simply underestimated Lian's strength,' said Grandfather. They might have seen every muscle in her body tense up, her head turning red in a matter of seconds, perhaps they even heard the crack as the grip of the sunshade burst in her hand. 'But they didn't see what I saw,' he said. They couldn't possibly have seen it from below—Lian's feet floating a tiny way, perhaps a sixteenth of an inch, above the rope. 'Most people,' Grandfather explained, 'are sadly always a little too weak for their own weight.' And that was exactly what kept us all on the ground, he told us. Only Lian was so strong that she could lift herself up in the air. That was why she'd always had to eat so much, he said. 'Otherwise she'd have kept floating off.'

Step by step, Lian ventured forward, her robe—still clutched at its seam by the acrobats—stretching behind her like a long white shadow. Grandfather glanced over at Hu, who was clinging to the platform's flimsy railing, but as soon as he caught Grandfather's eye he smiled proudly.

Lian had almost reached the midpoint of the wire and the entire audience was still holding its collective breath, all mouths agape, all movements frozen, absolute silence in the auditorium. The only noise was the swishing sound of Lian's thighs as they brushed against each other with every step.

When she was only about five yards away from Grandfather, the acrobats on the other side awoke from their catatonic astonishment, climbed down the ladder as fast as they could, ran across the stage and clambered up to Grandfather's platform. Only Hu remained on the other side, holding his hands in front of his eyes but still smiling.

Our food had grown cold; not one of us had taken a bite. Dai kept moving closer and closer to Grandfather, clutching at his arm although she already knew the story.

'Lian was only four or five steps away from me,' said Grandfather. 'And all of a sudden I was certain she'd make it.' The acrobats began pushing and shoving from behind him, stretching out their arms. The audience couldn't help leaping up from their seats, one after another venturing up to the edge of the stage, children sitting on their parents' shoulders, absolute strangers holding hands. 'Two more steps,' said Grandfather. 'I could smell Lian, I saw every burst vein in her eyes.' She took another step, Grandfather too now reaching his hand towards her, and all the bricks crumbled away from her gaze, the familiar deep well now freed again to fizz with effervescence. Lian raised her left foot for her final step, her fingertips touching Grandfather's hand.

'The cheers broke out a tenth of a second too early,' said Grandfather, splintering the chopstick between his fingers, 'just one damn tenth of a second.' Everyone clapped, everyone yelled, everyone stamped their feet and whistled on their fingers, the entire building vibrating, and the shock must have made Lian lose the tautness in her body for one minuscule flash. Her right foot dropped onto the wire, instantly tearing it, Lian waved her arms helplessly, the acrobats grabbed Grandfather from behind, Lian fell and clutched Grandfather's outstretched hand at the very last moment. Never had he held such a weight—it immediately tore him down too, and he would have plummeted hopelessly to the ground along with Lian, had the acrobats not pulled him back with all their might. Lian dangled below him. 'She didn't look up at me, she didn't struggle, all she did was release my hand finger by finger with great deliberation.' And as she began to slip he turned his arm with a swift movement and now it was he who grabbed Lian's hand, his fingers clawing so deeply into its soft flesh that they broke her skin in several places, and the blood on his fingertips, he said, was 'pleasantly cool'.

There was a cracking all through Grandfather's body; tendons and muscles seemed to be ripping. Lian screamed something—'She says you have to let her go,' Hu shouted from the other side, his voice cracking too, and Grandfather shouted that he wouldn't let go, never. The acrobats pulled at him as hard as they could but he was still slipping further and further over the edge of the platform. Lian screamed up to him again—'She says you have to let her go at last,' Hu translated. 'She says she's going to die anyway.'

'But so am I,' Grandfather called back, his whole body now hanging in mid-air, the pain in his arm now well past bearable.

Now Lian shouted her words directly at Hu. 'She says,' he translated, 'you were going to see what you could do about that.'

The acrobats only had him by his ankles now, and something ripped in his left arm. 'I take that back,' and Lian looked at him out of huge eyes. 'And then they got smaller all at once,' Grandfather told us, 'smaller and smaller, until they were nothing but two black dots.' And Lian's whole body got smaller too, moving away from him at breakneck speed although he was still holding her tight—that was the last thing he saw before he fainted.

'Two days later I woke up in hospital,' said Grandfather, rubbing the stump of his left arm. Of course he'd run straight out of the building, ignoring all the doctors' warnings, but he'd found no one at the Tamtam. The entire building had been empty and he'd found nothing there, not one forgotten panstick, and certainly not an arm.

The waiter cleared away our untouched plates. By that time Dai was practically sitting on Grandfather's lap. 'I'm going to bed,' he said quietly and got to his feet. Dai followed him, and when I went upstairs a few minutes later it was clear which of the two rooms was meant for me.

It's almost light again now. I have to get some sleep for a few hours, a few days, a few weeks.

Good night,

K.

'Pardon?' said the pathologist.

'It's not him,' I said. 'I don't know this man.' I tried to make it sound determined, added a little relief into my voice, a little incredulous amazement, even a tiny bit of faux regret that I couldn't be of more help to her.

The pathologist looked at me dubiously. She knew moments like this were an enormous emotional strain, she said. 'But are you quite sure this isn't your grandfather?'

I cast another deliberately casual glance at the unduly familiar corpse. 'Quite sure,' I said, and did she think I wouldn't recognize my own grandfather?

'And what about the arm?' she asked, she asked almost frantically, as if I owed her an explanation for this ostensible misunderstanding. She even unzipped the body bag a little further, revealing my grandfather's wide, white-haired chest, the scar from his bypass as if drawn on in felt-tip pen, the stump of his left arm so smooth and round that the right arm looked like a strange growth in comparison.

We never found his stump repulsive as children. On the contrary, we couldn't get enough of admiring and touching it, seeking solace there whenever we had worries. He'd roll up his left sleeve and patiently let us stroke the leathery bulge one after another. 'I'm afraid I've only got one,' he'd say.

I felt a sudden need to reach my hand out to it now, too, just to touch the stump briefly. I had to fold my arms behind my back to stop myself from giving in to that craving. 'It's the wrong arm,' I said quickly to the pathologist, even giving a brief laugh. 'It seems you made a mistake on the telephone. My grandfather's missing his right arm.'

The pathologist still didn't know what to make of what I'd said. She zipped up the body bag angrily, too fast for me to take a last look at my grandfather, and I couldn't let her notice what spread across my chest at a mad speed, what pushed its way up into my throat, what shot into my fingertips and tugged at my knees. All this here was my farewell after all and it wasn't about last looks or about whispered words or about swift kisses to blood-drained lips, it was about my grandfather. For the very last time it was all about him.

'Are you certain your grandfather's all right?' the pathologist asked after pushing the stretcher back into the refrigerator.

'I think so,' I said. 'He's travelling at the moment. But according to everything I've heard from him, he's doing just fine.'

'When did you last hear from him?' She wasn't going to let me off easily.

'A few weeks ago,' I said. 'But that doesn't mean anything. He's never written very often.'

She led me back out to the corridor. 'But there's the postcard.' Could I come and have a quick look at it?

I had hoped she'd forget that. I wanted to get out of there as soon as possible, I wanted to be out in the fresh air; I wouldn't be able to keep up my show of indifference for much longer. But I nodded. What else could I do? The pathologist popped into another room, came out with the postcard and handed it to me.

The front of the card was a photo of fir trees. There was nothing crossed out, not a trace of China. The writing on the back was widely spaced, the familiar illegible symbols. I looked for the 'You should have come with me' but didn't find it. 'Keith Stapperpf' was written in the address space, nothing more. The pathologist hadn't told me that on the phone.

'What makes you think it's addressed to me?' I asked. The pathologist gave a tired smile. They'd checked that, of course. I was the only person in the whole of Germany whose name started that way.

'And in America?' I asked. 'In Greece, in Argentina, in China? Did you check that as well?'

'No,' she said, but that was highly unlikely. Her smile got more and more tired. She didn't believe a word I was saying but I was used to that. 'Unlikely,' I said. 'Do you know what's unlikely? It's unlikely that a man with a missing arm is in here who still isn't my grandfather. It's unlikely that he has a half-written postcard with him addressed to someone with a name similar to mine. It's unlikely that that man didn't have any papers on him. It's unlikely that you're so suntanned. It's unlikely that I'm in China, that's even highly unlikely, and the most unlikely thing is that I'm about to get married.' And all of a sudden I couldn't help laughing, I couldn't stop laughing, there were tears running down my face, I gasped for air, the pathologist gave me a confused look, which only made me laugh even more, I could only ever stop for a few seconds and then it came snorting out of me again, my whole body trembled, my stomach muscles hurt, and I was incredibly exhausted, and I was incredibly relieved and presumably incredibly moved, seeing as I was trying to hug the pathologist, which she managed to prevent. She pushed me away with both hands. 'Thank you very much for coming,' she said and propelled me towards the door. I was sorry I hadn't been able to help her, I said. The pathologist shrugged. 'If it does occur to you that you know the man from somewhere, do get in touch straight away please.'

'Of course,' I said, but I knew that wouldn't happen; I knew the man well enough for that.

I'd already got halfway along the corridor when the pathologist came chasing after me. 'The postcard,' she said, reaching out a hand, and for a moment I thought about simply running off, running as fast as I could, out of the hospital, onto a bus that might be just leaving, and I'd watch out of the window as the pathologist halted, hands on her hips, got smaller and smaller until she finally vanished, and I'd be out of breath, pressing the rescued postcard to my chest and not letting go.

But, of course, then I'd have given everything away, of course the postcard wouldn't be in safety, I wouldn't be in safety and least of all my grandfather. I handed it back to the pathologist. 'Did you read what it says?' I asked as casually as possible.

'I tried,' she said, and then she walked slowly back along the corridor. 'Say hello to your grandfather from me,' she called after me, not turning round.

On the train back home I retrieved the yellow note I'd put in my pocket in the house a few hours earlier, and I held it up to the window, but that was no use either in deciphering the traces of the previous message on it. I opened the lid of the small ashtray next to my seat, ran my finger along the inside of it, rubbed the grey dust across the note and the letters stood out in yellow. I was disappointed; I knew the message already, it had been attached to my younger sister's old tutu that morning. 'Isn't this much too tight for you?' it said. Even there, the words had annoyed me. My grandfather always had to stick his nose in everything, he always had to state his opinion on everything. And now on the train, the words annoyed me even more because they were obviously the last thing he'd wanted to tell us. No 'Goodbye,' no 'Don't wait for me,' no dramatic 'I'll give the cat your regards.' Just 'Isn't this much too tight for you?'—as if it really was nothing more than a trip he was embarking on, as if he'd be back soon to stick his nose into everything again. I could only hope that this nondescript message was all part of his plan, the plan I now believed I had carried out on his behalf. He simply hadn't allowed himself any final farewells—he was just on a trip, we'd merely lost sight of him for a while.

I screwed up the yellow note and threw it in the ashtray. I'd be home in half an hour; the appointment at the registry office was at three, and all of a sudden I was incredibly tired, all of a sudden nothing seemed urgent any more, nothing but sleeping. And that was just what I'd do, I'd go straight to the garden house as soon as the train arrived, I'd lie down and hope I wouldn't wake up until the next day.

24 May, near Fenghuang

My dears,

To my left lies a trapeze artiste, to my right a lady contortionist, both asleep, and I too am actually far too
exhausted to write, but so much happened today that I
want to tell you about, even though the days are beginning
to blur together, even though they seem like years to me.

I was woken this morning by loud noises from the
next room. I opened the window, switched on the televi-
sion and turned up the volume but it was no use, so I went
down for an early breakfast. Grandfather and Dai didn't
join me until midday. They were in a fine mood, Grandfather even hugged me, and Dai kissed me on the cheek. 'So,
did you sleep well?' I asked.

Grandfather ignored all my undertones and said, 'Very
well,' and told me he was starving. Dai ordered far too
much again, of course.

'Help yourself,' they kept telling me, but I simply
shook my head, taking one cigarette after the next out of
Dai's pack and trying to cough as little as possible, while
Grandfather and Dai fed each other bites of food. Didn't
we have to get a move on, I asked once it all got too much
for me. If I'd understood rightly we still had something to
do, I said, or wasn't that so important any more now?

Grandfather dabbed at his mouth with his napkin.
'Yes, it is,' he said quietly, of course it was, arranging a

couple of grains of rice on the edge of his bowl. 'What if Hu can't remember me?' he asked, and Dai took his hand. Of course he would, she said, what with all that had happened back then. Grandfather nodded. 'Yes,' he said. 'Let's hope it did happen.'

Outside the hostel Dai got us a new car, an SUV— we'd need it, she said. I sat on the spacious back seat, a good six feet away from the front seats, and so once again I could hardly make out what the two of them were cooing and whispering. It probably wasn't meant for my ears anyway. I heard them laughing every few seconds, sometimes I saw Dai slapping Grandfather in jest, and sometimes her hand stayed on his side for longer and I quickly looked out of the window.

We soon left the city wall behind us and were driving through almost untouched scenery. Forests stretched away from the dusty road on either side, hundreds of chalk hills protruding from between the treetops, huge caves gaping on some of them. I had never seen anything like it—the green was so lush that it stung my eyes, waterfalls glinted everywhere in the sun, monkeys frolicked by the side of the road, and once Dai had to brake suddenly because a herd of elephants was crossing the street. Around twenty of them passed by at a leisurely pace, taking no notice of us. Only the last of them stopped right in front of the car, turned round to us and gave us a tired stare through the windscreen. His wrinkled eyes migrated from Dai to me and finally to Grandfather, where they rested for a long time, and suddenly the elephant raised its trunk, swung it sedately and tipped its head to one side. This went on for several minutes, none

of us daring to move, and then the beast lowered its trunk
and trotted into the woods.

'What on earth was that?' I asked.

'It looked like an invitation,' said Dai. Grandfather was
still sitting motionless and not saying a word. He remained
mute for the rest of the journey, while Dai cast concerned
glances in his direction now and then. 'He must have mis-
taken you for someone else.'

A few hours later we turned off the road and onto a
small woodland track. Now I understood why we needed
the SUV. Roots and branches grew over the roadway, which
we could barely make out after a few yards anyway. I had
no idea how Dai managed to find the way here; we were
driving deeper and deeper into the woods but at some
point the trees grew sparser and we found ourselves on a
grassy space, in the middle of it a huge four-storey building. Dai switched off the engine. 'I don't think this can be
the right place,' said Grandfather, peering sceptically over
at the house. Dai didn't answer. She strode swiftly over to
the entrance and I pushed Grandfather after her. A sign
next to the door in a good dozen languages read 'Home
for Incapacitated Artistes (doctor's note required)'.

'Are you ready?' I asked Grandfather.

'No,' he said, took a deep breath and rang the bell.

In a matter of seconds, a small man in a red leotard
opened the door. He seemed out of breath and cast only a
brief glance at us, then turned round again and began
backflipping along the hallway at breathtaking speed,
stumbling every few seconds, getting up with a curse, rubbing his elbows and starting off again.

We followed him. The hallway branched off a few times and then opened out into a kind of gym. It's almost impossible to describe the hustle and bustle that presented itself there. Artistes of all kinds were practising their feats and tricks in a wild confusion, and none of them seemed to work. We saw weightlifters trapped on the floor beneath their dumb-bells, we saw soot-blackened fire-eaters, we saw tightrope walkers trembling before low stools, we saw a sword swallower with a host of blades poking out of his belly. There was a net halfway across the hall in which some of the trapeze artists were wriggling, others constantly failing to catch each other above our heads, clowns were stuck in cannons, conjurers were shaking their empty top hats in rage, and the floor was littered with juggling balls and thrown knives.

Grandfather and I watched it all with mouths agape but Dai seemed unmoved, simply smiling sadly. 'It's just like it used to be,' she said, and then she leant down to a hopelessly tangled contortionist and asked her something, and the snake-woman somehow managed to extract her right arm from beneath her left calf and pointed to a door on one side of the room. Dai turned back to us. 'Hu is in his office,' she said and looked at Grandfather. He nodded.

Outside the office, he ran his hand through his hair a few more times. Dai knocked, there was a croak from inside, and we entered.

At first glance there was no sign of Hu. It was only after a few seconds that I spotted him, almost entirely hidden by a desk in a corner by the window. Everything seemed too large for him—the chair he was sitting on, his suit with its sleeves hanging well beyond his hands, even his skin didn't fit him, hung thin and stained over his skull as if to dry. He blinked at us, then got to his feet, came towards us with tiny steps and examined Dai's face, which she leant down to him, through a magnifying glass. 'Dai,' he croaked happily, and he hugged her and the two of them exchanged a few excited words until Dai finally whispered something in his ear. Hu froze. He looked cautiously up at Grandfather, took a step closer and ran the magnifying glass over his face, touching it with one hand and then grabbing at the left sleeve dangling empty at Grandfather's side. And all at once his small body began to tremble so hard that I feared for a moment he would collapse before our very eyes. Hu clutched at Grandfather's sleeve, shook it, pressed it to his chest, and then the trembling subsided and Hu cleared his throat. 'The world sensation Lian would say now that I'm overjoyed to see you again.' Dai wiped her eye and I too was more moved than I'd imagined.

Only Grandfather seemed strangely restrained. He merely shifted from one foot to the other, looking round at Dai for help, and when Hu asked him how he had been since back then, he said, 'Quite well, all considered.' There was soon an awkward silence. Hu let go of Grandfather's sleeve and played round with his magnifying glass in embarrassment. We didn't want to take up too much of his time, said Grandfather, and Hu gave a hasty nod.

'Just one moment please though,' he said and left the room, and Dai and I began reasoning with Grandfather. What was the matter with him, we asked, and wasn't he glad to have reached his destination now, and Grandfather interrupted us, he hadn't reached anything, nothing at all, least of all a destination. He still didn't know what he'd been looking for here, but all he'd found anyway was a small man, just as everything was smaller than it used to be, just as everything was shrinking, getting smaller and smaller all the time, and in the end it would only be visible through a magnifying glass. So it ought to just disappear altogether.

'Let's go,' said Grandfather, and at that moment Hu came back, carrying a long glass container in which something sloshed to and fro.

He pressed it into Grandfather's hand. 'I've been keeping this for you.'

And then I saw it. The arm was floating in a cloudy liquid, the broken bone poking out at the top, the fingers crooked, even the scratches on the back of the hand visible. Grandfather held the jar away from him hesitantly, as if he was supposed to look after it for a moment, but then all at once he began to sob, his shoulders collapsed and he pressed his head to the glass, the arm moving slowly up and down behind it only an inch away from his face, and now we could clearly see that it was the arm of a young man. Should we leave him alone for a moment, asked Dai. Grandfather nodded and we tiptoed out of the room. Before I closed the door he turned round to me one more time. 'I'm not holding on to her any more,' he said, and he smiled.

Hu insisted we stay for dinner and spend the night there. 'What better reason to celebrate,' he said, 'than when old friends and body parts meet again.'

Grandfather was the star of the evening, of course. Hu said he'd told his artistes the story over and over, and now they crowded round him, every one of them wanting to be close to him and to hear the story again from his own lips, but Grandfather refused them with a wave of his hand. 'I can't remember it all exactly,' he claimed.

The female artistes were particularly stubborn. Would he like to feed them potatoes, they asked, or perhaps he'd like to see their tightrope acts, and a few courageous souls even asked to touch the stump of his left arm, but Grandfather shook his head politely and retired to his room early with Dai. 'My grandson will keep you company,' were his parting words. 'He takes after me.' And for the first time, those words didn't bother me.

It turned out to be a long evening, and now I can hardly keep my eyes open, my dears.

Although Grandfather sees it differently, some kind of destination has been reached. It feels good, even though it means we'll have to see what to do next.

How are you all anyway?

Best wishes,

K.

The crowbar used to break open the lock of the garden house had been abandoned on the ground and the door swung loosely in its splintered frame. I opened it with two fingers.

Franziska was sitting on the desk. She was wearing her blue raincoat, her legs were crossed and she held her phone in her left hand, a cigarette burning in her right hand. Next to her was a messy pile of the letters I'd written to my brothers and sisters. She didn't look my way when I walked in but pressed a few buttons on her phone. A moment later my telephone started ringing under the desk, and after the fifth ring the answering machine switched on as usual. 'Special K, are you there?' asked Franziska, and when I didn't react she said, 'What a shame, I wanted to tell you in person but now I'll just have to do it this way.' She still wasn't looking at me. She pulled a new cigarette out of the box with her lips and lit it with the glowing stub in her hand before she flicked it to the floor. 'By the time you hear this you'll know I wasn't at the registry office,' she said. 'You'll know I didn't marry you,' she said. 'You'll have waited outside the entrance with one of those ridiculous cheap bouquets. You'll have paced up and down and asked everyone who walked past for the time, some of them many times. Then you'll have gone up to room 208 or whatever it was but I won't have been there either, and the registrar will have looked rather impatient, and no, he won't have heard anything from me either. You'll have called me from his telephone but as you know I didn't answer. "She's always forgetting her phone," you'll have said to the registrar and you'll have laughed in that funny way and he'll have shrugged and . . .'

My answering machine beeped, Franziska took a drag on her cigarette and then pressed redial, waited for the message and continued, 'You'll have made a pretty couple, the registrar and you, him watering his plants while you kept trying to get hold of me. Perhaps something had happened to me, he'll have said, and it was probably meant to sound reassuring. And it'll all have been terribly embarrassing for you, even though the registrar will have assured you it happens all the time and it's more of an exception when both partners do turn up. He'll even have offered you a coffee, with a dash of something stronger, and on your second cup you'll have left the coffee out of it altogether, and you'll have got rather chatty as usual. You'll have told the poor man the whole story about me and you and your grandfather, in far too much detail of course, and you'll have kept topping up your rum, and the registrar will have kept on nodding and saying "I see," and sometimes "Goodness me," and in the end you'll have looked him in the eye, as best you could after all that rum, and he'll have been slurring his words too and he'll have said I was really a fascinating woman but he wouldn't marry me for all the money in the world. "You should be glad she didn't turn up," he'll have said, and then you'll have embraced awkwardly, and you'll . . .'

The answering machine interrupted her again, and this time Franziska took her time redialling. She finished her cigarette, she looked out of the window, she rubbed at a mark on her coat and only then did she make the next call. The phone rang again under the desk, once, twice, and then I got down on my knees, crawled over to the telephone and picked up after the fourth ring. 'Hello?' I asked.

'It's me, Franziska,' she said.

'Franziska,' I said. 'Did you just try calling?'

'Once or twice maybe,' she said, and then we both fell silent. But Franziska falls silent faster than other people so she was soon finished. 'How are you?' she asked.

'Very well, thanks.'

'Good,' said Franziska, and told me she was glad to hear that.

'Where are you calling from?' I asked.

She cleared her throat. 'From China,' she said then, 'I'm in China.'

I looked up at the night sky drawn above me, the sickle moon, the randomly ordered planets. 'That's a coincidence,' I said. 'That's where I am too.'

'You don't say,' said Franziska.

'And you won't believe all the things that have happened here,' I said.

'Oh I will,' said Franziska, 'I probably will.'

I looked at the radio alarm clock, the washing-up sponges, the answering machine with its flashing digits. 'Who knows, maybe we'll bump into each other,' I said. I heard her lighting a new cigarette and I ran my fingers over the buttons on the answering machine. 'Delete all,' it said next to one of them, and I pressed it.

'Yes, who knows. That's easy enough in China,' said Franziska. It was twenty to three. I had to put the letters to my brothers and sisters in the letterbox before they got home; maybe I'd even manage to draw Chinese postmarks on the envelopes. Franziska drummed her fingers on the tabletop from above. It sounded like rain. 'I think I can see you already,' I said and hung up.

25 May, China

My dears,

I don't have much time left to write, I'm afraid. One of Hu's assistants has offered to take me with him to Fenghuang in a minute because he has a few things to get done there. He can post the letters there for me too, he said and he admitted it might be 'sometimes rather difficult for foreigners'.

Grandfather woke me at the crack of dawn. He just wanted to say a quick goodbye, he said, and I looked at him, still half asleep, and asked what he meant, and Grandfather pushed the sleeping trapeze artiste's leg aside and sat down on the edge of the bed. Dai and he were leaving now, he said. They'd decided it last night. Dai was going to hand in her notice at the bank and start training, she was sure to pick up a few of her old acts soon enough, and he himself would freshen up the shoelace trick, conjuring was like riding a bike, you never forget how to do it, and in a few weeks' time they wanted to go from town to town together, playing at small variety theatres, and maybe on the streets now in the summer. They could sleep al fresco and barbecue crayfish on their campfire by night. 'You know,' he said, 'my famous thyme crayfish.' They'd go further and further east until they got to the mountains; Dai wanted to show him those most of all. 'She says it's so quiet by night in the mountains you can hear your own hair growing,' whispered

Grandfather, 'and I'd like to give that a try once in my lifetime.'

I sat up in bed. When was he thinking of coming back, I asked. There was no reply. But he would be coming back, I asked, and Grandfather gave my arm a brief stroke. 'I've got to go now,' he said.

Dai was waiting by the car. She gave me a long hug and then she got in the car, Grandfather sitting next to her in the passenger seat. He still had the plane tickets, I said, and Grandfather found them in his wallet, looked at them for a moment and handed them to me through the window. 'Isn't this much too tight for you?' he asked. Dai started the engine, the car drove off to the edge of the clearing and then the forest swallowed it up, and I realized I'd forgotten to wave.

I looked at the tickets in my hand. The return flight is booked for tomorrow. I don't think I'll take it. It really is much too tight for me. Everything's much too tight for me at the moment, and perhaps I'll just keep on going, have a bit more of a look round. It's a big country after all.

See you soon.

All best,

K.

Everything that happens to correspond to the truth in the descriptions is taken from the travel guide *Lonely Planet China*.